WHERE THE DEAD GO

A Novel

RASA SAMIMI

Copyright © 2021 Rasa Samimi

All rights reserved under International and Pan-American Copyright Conventions. No part of this book may be reproduced in any form or by any electronic or mechanical means, without permission in writing from the author, except by a reviewer, who may quote brief passages in a review.

Zeba Publishing

ISBN: 978-0-9938236-3-3

In memory of Jax

Contents

"We have found a strange footprint on the shores of the unknown. We have devised profound theories, one after another, to account for its origins. At last, we have succeeded in reconstructing the creature that made the footprint. And lo! it is our own."

~ Sir Arthur Stanley Eddington

First Death

THE DEAD GO to Earth's dark matter doppelgänger lurking in the space all round us; wherein we live on till a second death (with a few exceptions which manage to solve the great riddle of being). This is the account of that: a crossing to the secreted realms of the dead, there and back again.

~

ADAM CAME to a furore of undulating mountainous seas. Jolted aback at being not in Flora's arms dying; then, by a silhouette of a woman with a thrashed hair flash across. The buoyant force of a monstrous wave borne him straight up and down like a cork. Flaccid stiffs darted about gigantic maëlströms—vortices cork-screwing the dead—funnelling the newborn—down to an aethe-real abyss.

All around, in the midst of gargantuan swells and swirls, vortexes in breadths of the mightiest of vessels stretched flappy forms in terrific funnels out of sight. Out of the blue, Adam's feet fluttered, and a sinuous undercurrent crept up—up and up over his sinewy body, seized, and yanked him to the nearest ström. Quaking head-to-toe, Adam slipped into a tortuous tempest-toss. Flushed round and round, he flip-flopped on, on, down. Coiling serpentine-like this way and that while whisked ever inward to the gyre's eye. With the power of a struggle ripped fast from him while he stomached the churn of a non-stop whirling grind.

Adam fancied eternity lapse in a continual gyring bent to go on ad nauseam. But the rapid sweeping descent did come to an abrupt jerking halt beyond a next bend. He opened his lids, one by vertiginous one, to a quasi-unearthly scene: adrift in the core of a maelstrom. Encompassed, as far as the eye could fathom it, in a dizzily interlacing spiralling rampart of waters. From outside its vertex a blazing glow bathed the cone in prismatic light to the curl's pointy bottom. Drops teared and tossed out of the writhing braiding helix in concentric wreaths and hung aloft, riveting him. An eerie deafened hush reigned inside the eye of the ström. Mill-streams don't make a swish, Adam reckoned, unbelieving. Then, an arresting devil-sent insight swept over him to restore his self-possession. He was not breathing. He grasped he had not an urge to breathe till its notion flitted through his mind: prompting him to gape his mouth and, in heaves, gasp gulps of that chunnel's air. At that instant, the hovering ringing droplets dropped, all at once, like a curtain. Then, Adam fell. Plunged to a breathtaking rush. Nosedived the eye of the psychedelically wringing twirl at some heart-stopping terminal velocity that ceased his heart. (Nay though. Adam is not certain if his heart had *had* been beating all along so to stop therefor.)

As he plummeted in the bole of the whorl Adam noticed its circumference falling in degrees with quick thrusts and feared its circumvolution unravelling on him. But at its bottom the ström's conscribing waters drain out of a hole as a waterspout. So, after a further fall down a spout, then, a fleeting well, and tailspins in a below-ground waterfall, Adam slapped, splashed, and sank in a pool.

The sharp sink stunned him; he just about passed out from a rush of blood to his head and by the stinging smack at the pool's surface. Even so, he did not lose his presence of mind. Sunk to a depth of about twenty metres, with frenetic kicks and strokes, he surfaced, wheezing, in a cavernous granite chamber. The well he had fell from was way, way up in a conical ceiling, out of which cataracts cascaded in gyred sheets down to a spray or cast along granite walls to a concave basin. An astounding volume of water, pouring in jugful, coursed through Adam's ruddy face: salt-and-pepper hair and beard. Squinting up to the protracted well in the cavern's top (a colossus telescope now) he made out a wee grey patch.

Now, an ear-splitting din of a half moan, half whistle—such as the gales of a hurricane pressured through the chinks of some thousand-thousand drafty doors, windows, and airducts—rang in the hollow; unsettling, frightful, long-drawn-out shrieks and hisses like some shrill cries of pissed off beasts and, or witches. The sulphurous wisps of air in there begot a taste of cooked eggs.

Adam trod water, rotated in the pool, gazed all around, and found himself in a wondrous subterranean labyrinthine. He saw canals fanning out of the four corners of the pool under domed granite passageways lit by rows of round, red lamps strung up like beads that gleam and glitter; with each channel issuing to another pool in another vast cavity with a dreadful waterfall and waterways that spread out from the corners of those pools: and so on, and so forth.

Wide-eyed, Adam spotted a tall bald man, garbed in a grey frock and a reed-like staff, hasten to the chamber from an archway. A circlet of a stitch-curved red lettering on the left breast pocket of the man's ballooning frock marked him as a Necropolis Watchmen.

Upon seeing Adam, the Watchman became perplexed, pale. Gestured with the mimed pressings of the palm of his free hand outward while mouthing "*Stay*". And then turned to rush up that gallery's stairs: to return awhile whence with another man in-toe. The other man had had a puffed-up countenance. Irreproachably attired: In velvety black frock and gloves. With his shiny-as-poss coal-black hair combed flat to a side. Clasping wire-framed sunglasses. Short-to-medium in girth and clad in an over-ample robe he wore the signs he stocked a considerable muscular might and slunk the steps in the stretched, determined strides of a soldierly man.

While gesturing to the Watchman with one hand, without a glance downward, the man spread his other hand to show Adam the pool's half-submerged steps. (Like he seemed to see without looking.) Adam saw the stone steps thru a sheet of water pouring over a protrusion overhanging the steps and followed the man's gist.

In a wink, two consecutive splashes kicked up waves in the pool. After a beat, a man's body plopped out on the surface like a log; then, a sun-bronzed body of an old woman bobbed along. Adam had never swum as quick as he swam to that pool's steps. Stepping thru that glassy waterfall, Adam, seeing his nakedness, had stopped up short and scissored his arms and legs in shame. Adam's brawny body was as red and as crinkly as a baked apple. He had the pins and needles and heard a crackle and pop jangle. He looked about him for a place to hide, all twisted and troubled.

The Watchman came and swaddled Adam's shaking frame with a green blanket. A red flaked stencilled imprint branded the rather long, rather prickly blanket as the Property of Necropolis Military.

The Watchman fussed over the lay of the blanket on Adam. Then went to finger earplugs in Adam's ears, which led Adam to snap his head in and to hunch his torso: from feeling the Watchman's slithering fingers graze his ears and tingle out his goose-flesh, evermore. The long-limbed Watchman stepped over and held up the earplugs to show his intention as Adam straightened up.

The Watchman wasn't old, nor, for that matter, young. With a see-through skin; bulging nose; a puffy, protruding lower lip; big, gray eyes; and, with strange protuberances on his head and face. Moreover, there was something peculiar, or else, torturous about him. Maybe, gloomy, in a queer, religious sense. Perhaps his demeanour had had the manifestation of exhaustion or utter suffering.

Once Adam had raised his head, he caught the Watchman's eye for an instant. There was a fraction of a moment when their eyes had met, and, straight off, Adam knew that the Watchman was bidding to convey a message. It was as though their minds had melded, and the thoughts were passing through their eyes. *I can help you*, the Watchman appeared to be imparting. And then, therefrom, the intelligence drop switched off as the dilating eyes of the Watchman darted from Adam's brown eyes to the black-robed man, then back. The Watchman brandished the earplugs, again. (This time wearing a deadpan mien.) And with Adam's nods of consent the Watchman set in the earplugs. With Adam's endeavour at catching an eye, once more, prompting the Watch-man into diverting his eyes, once again. Nonetheless, Adam was convinced, the Watchman, without doubt, had passed on a brain-wave. (*If* he had telepathized, in fact.)

Here, the black-frocked man led Adam to the gallery's staircase, with the Watchman staying back—with a concerned look. An icy drizzle draped the dank cavern, and its floor waxed wet, stony, and tacky beneath Adam's bare feet. In the trice of black-robed man's peeps back Adam took in a clean-shaven chiselled face: unblemished and rose-coloured like the newborns. And the blackened irises of his narrow eyes with the flicker of that wild, jittery motion which in apt wanders in the eyes of madmen; and looked away at once since those roused eyes penetrated Adam's skull.

Stepping on the stairway Adam noticed nature had formed the pathway: forged by a lava stream thrusting a flight through, creäting a steep, inclined plane long ago; with its residual ripples carved to serve the place of steps; with a drop on each side of its ramp. At the top step of the stair a red door slid open, and a fierce flash shone Adam to a squint as he hoofed into an aslant, rough-hewn rock-chamber. As his eyes adjusted to the glare, he made out twin flickering buzzing neon tubes on a low, uneven ceiling; a row of glistening elevators on a side; and a couple of cast-iron chairs at the ends of an oblong wrought iron table sat across the cave.

The black-robed man stamped in—the red door shut with a whoosh—waved Adam to a chair; went down the table to sit on a chair; and then pulled his earplugs out. Adam followed suit. Whereafter the man spoke with a hiss thru his teeth like that of a snake.

"My name's Nacash Abaddon, Mr...?"
Adam did not recall his own name. He strained to remember it. He turned vexed, then, angry, because he could not remember it.

Then, his mouth opened, and, in a bass tone, he voiced out "A—dam—ah," like his name did not belong to him.

"Ah! Adamah! Mr Adamah. Greetings! Greetings..." Nacash Abaddon carried on, in a particularizing, half talking to himself manner, as he placed his sunglasses on the table; with the wrought iron table bedewed with drops that each bore that scene all trembling as though they had been frightened by something.

"Adamah... That's..., biblical, isn't it?"

"Well—"

"—It *is!*"

"Well—"

"—Believe it's..., Hebrew. Signifying the red colour of *earth*, dust or nothingness. Or Farsi for: human beings."

"I—"

"—Break up the name Adam, Adam—you go by the shortened version, *Adam*, do you not, Mr Adamah?"

"Yes, I—"

"—Well, break up *Adam* into its two syllables and what do you get? Why! it reads, *a dam*; as in, an obstruction!"

Eyeballing his distorted reflection on the sunglasses, Adam became suspicious of Nacash Abaddon's aim in furnishing these points off of his name. Seeing how as Nacash Abaddon spoke he was watching every look that rose on Adam's face as though he was bidding to elicit a particular tell in each one of them.

"Why are you telling me all this, Mr..."

"Nacash Abaddon," he resaid, dropped his eyes, and beetled his brows; and then hastened to restore his facial expression to a more befitting façade: let out a rustle of a laugh: and picked up a put-on cheerful manner. "See here my good man, that all was to quicken the linguistic muscle, one's wit, with a good airing; that's all it was. Meant no disrespect. Say! erm, were you awake, er—

er, *conscious*..., through the whole ordeal?" Nacash Abaddon rattled on, tongue-a-wagging; and glanced over his shoulders and switched to an undertone: suggestive of more than only common curiosity: as though he was attempting to suss out some secret.

"What ordeal?" questioned Adam, sneaking a peek behind his own shoulders.

"*What ordeal?*" echoed an exasperated Nacash Abaddon.

"Yes; what ordeal?" re-echoed Adam, agitated.

"*Hiss!*" Nacash Abaddon hissed. "*There,*" he posed, gesticulating rumble-tumbles with fingers spun upwards. "*Sky Ocean...*"

"I'm not—not sure...," Adam started, hesitated, and, thus, began to commune with himself: Wriggling like a worm cut in two. Scratching his head as if Nacash Abaddon had lain a puzzle. Then he spied the breast pocket of Nacash Abaddon's black frock with the skeleton of a red dragon with seven heads sewn into it. "Sorry, who did you say you are?" Adam asked, as he continued to gaze at the man's pocket; wiggling his chair closer to the table to peer at seven crowns and ten horns beseamed on top of the red dragonet's seven skulls.

"Nacash Abaddon! How many times do I need to repeat my name to you, eh, *Adam*?" he snarled a slobbered-out tongue-lashing.

"What I mean is: Who are you? What do you do here?"

"Ah! O, forgive me," Nacash Abaddon reacted in a pseudo-conciliatory about-face. "I'm the Keeper of world's Necropolis."

"Am I..., dead?" Adam dreaded, with a quavering voice, a raised, dimpled chin, pressed lips, and furrowed brows.

"How could you be dead, eh? You were just born!" Nacash Abaddon cried out in a venomous rapture, forbearing his prairie-dogging tongue; then rustled out a soundless laugh with a wide-open mouth and a soughing throat while he fanned about a hand.

"*Born*? Born to what—where?"

"O THE WORLD!" boomed Nacash Abaddon; then threw in a delayed sweep of a drawn-out hand at a side of the barren cave. But, next, he fizzed in through his teeth. And, with his blackened irises quivering, he whispered to a bowed aside: "*Before the five-month incubation period, which hasn't happened before—once—hist!*" Halted (as he had become conscious of his self-talk); hiccoughed; pushed out of his seat, declared, "I must go now," and hustled to leave. Caught by Nacash Abaddon's abrupt leave-taking, Adam waggled out of his chair. And, as he swathed his body with the blanket, Nacash Abaddon strode across that chamber—with his characteristic taut footfalls—to the bank of the elevators to press their up button. And from there Nacash Abaddon extended up a flat-handed arm, along with an askance eye, to proscribe Adam from speaking, as he pounded back to the table to pocket the sunglasses which he had almost left behind (with an added puff of a huff of a great relief).

"I realize you may have many unanswered questions, Mr Adamah—too many for me to address at the moment—am sure," Nacash Abaddon resumed with an assumed air of regret. "But I'm certain you will fall upon the answers to all your questions, soon enough. Starting with your passage out of Necropolis up to the subsurface of our spheroid. Now, if you'd please proceed to the bottom of those stairs, the Watchman shall guide you in your passage into our world," Nacash Abaddon prescribed; and then stepped into an elevator sliding its water-drip-veined door. And, as the draggled door of the elevator re-rolled, Nacash Abaddon cast Adam a prolonged stare. But then hastened to say a hurried:

"That Watchman doesn't speak, eh; he's made a vow of—"

Left there, Adam felt in between a lunatic's *reverie mystifique* and a matter sober and real. He recalled dying moments before, yet, he was alive, still. Not in all his harebrained musings could he have dreamt up such a hereafter, Adam figured. His head was swimming....

It is farsighted to mention in parenthesis, however, that, at this juncture, Adam had not known what laid in the offing. For, a daring adventure out of the hiding places of wicked things—'for many be called, but few chosen'—had just then begun.

Chapter Two

Passage from Necropolis

THREE BLACK forms in black frocks and black helmets and black machine guns rushed the chamber and halted in front of Adam. One gave Adam a slight cuff and he fell backwards on his behind.

"Ow!" he groaned, struggling with the blanket under him. A muffled, devilish guffawing roared out of the featureless black glass of the three black helmets.

"Why did you do that?" yelled Adam, springing to feet with a face turning purplish crimson; clasping the blanket to his chin. The three black figures stepped forward, leaned in, and appeared to grow taller and even more startling.

"Whoa! Whoa! Whoa! What's going on here?" feared Adam, raising a hand.

The scene deformed back on the slick helmets.

A red jumpsuit hit Adam on the elbow and dropped to the floor.

The Black Helmets bristled—growled.

Adam's heart, pounding, just about jumped out of his chest.

"What? Want me to wear these overalls?" he squeaked out.

Getting those Black Helmets to say a word was like coaxing a cent out of an old penny pincher's pocket. So, Adam took their brooding noises for an aye, turned his back, and, under the cover of the green blanket over his shoulders, got in the red jumpsuit.

A thump on his back sent Adam flying headlong into a wall.

"Ai! Ai!" Adam wailed; staggered, grasped vainly at the wall, then slithered to the floor.

The Black Helmets moved in and doled out a flurry of kicks and blows with great zeal and fury. After a short halt, they stepped back. Curled up in the fetal position on the floor, Adam remained still.

Come to, Adam could see from under the lid of one eye; a bloody cloth wrapped his right eye. He was in a wheelchair moving in a dim shaft. A long chain wound round him from head to toe: from a ring on his neck to handcuffed wrists to padlocked ankles. He felt like boulders had crushed him. Each whack had marked him with a black-and-blue spot. Blood had run down his mouth and nose. Sharp pains jabbed at his ribs. A throb numbed his swollen nose. And he heaved sighs from the depth of his bowels. Dazed, Adam squinted about with his good eye with such an intensity that it seemed like he had lost all his marbles. He was rolling on a platform of a canal. A procession of shadows bent and leapt on up the curved in, jagged rock-walls with each passing red lamp. Two Black Helmets stomped in front, the Watchman pushed the wheelchair, and a third Black Helmet trailed as a rearguard. A Watchman, with a staff, poked at inanimate and all puckered up bodies afloat in a stream that sheened like a semi-molten glass. "Where are you guys taking me?" Adam, mortified, pled, which met with no response. As is normal for bound men to have loose tongues, Adam raged choice curses at those Black Helmets; they paid no mind.

They went down tube after tube, arch after arch, in twists and turns, here and there taking sharp turns to their right or left, up an underground maze. At one forking turn Adam saw a void, like a fox hole, a mere scoop, so narrow one would need to crawl into it, blocked with crisscrossed yellow tape and caution signs.

Jack-in-the-box unexpectedly, they came up on a great cave; a cavern two hundred and fifty feet high, by a hundred feet wide, which seemed to have split in two from a volcanic upheaval; with its grand, vaulted ceiling formed by some mighty force of nature. Warm air struck at Adam's face. Before him, a majestic hall, lit by a wide borehole slanted upward high above; its smooth, black granite walls glinted spotted golds. Beneath the hole, on top of a mass of stones and pebbles, wooden carts carted up and down a sharp incline in and out of the opening. At the foot of the tracks, split lines of women and men—boys and girls, in pink and blue onesies, formed. A big banner hung from the roof top exclaimed: WELCOME TO THE WORLD, NEWBORN!

As they rolled Adam into the hall turmoil came to his ears; a racket of howls and hee-haw, like at an unruly daycare, tolled. Nurses tried to soothe the distressed. A tearful man bolted out of the boy's line; a nearby Black Helmet guarding the cave chased the man round the hall, caught and slapped the man back in line. Then one of the tram conductors rang a handbell, called out, "ALL ABOARD!" and all that ruckus petered out since all were agog to ride in a trolley.

"Hup! boys and girls, in you go now," the conductor lulled. At that point, the stout conductor saw Adam and his entourage, gave a wink to the Watchman and stiff nods to the Black Helmets. Once all got in the caboose—plus a busty blond nurse with hard nipples—the conductor picked up an old-fashioned rotary phone handset and called out "Seventeen!" Then, he turned his neck to where they had placed Adam in the car, and added, "Plus one—in wheelchair. Yup. Nope. How should I know how much wheelchairs weight? Figure it out. Yup. Just start letting it out; and if it doesn't work, I will take him out," he said, and then slammed the handset. A fearful Adam chewed on what they were going to let out... After a short wait, with a jerk, the car set off its slow, steep climb. "Choo-Choo..." the jolly conductor sounded with pumps of his fist to the glee of those so-called newborn. A commotion of small pebbles rolled away at their feet at the track. The nurse set in train to tend to the newborn with pacifiers, baby bottles, and sippy cups. (Grown men and women glugging milk turned his stomach.)

When the nurse got to Adam, she went to shove a bottle in his mouth. Adam rucked his lips, shook his head, and objected with "I'm *not* a baby!"

"He can speak!" The nurse was positively flummoxed.

"Of course—" Adam started, but the butt of a machine gun whacked him in the jaw. A bloodied tooth flew out of his mouth and hit the nurse right in the eye. A streak of blood sprayed up her tight, white uniform. Gaping down at herself, she let out a yelp; then, she screamed; and screamed. After a beat all the newborn began to sob—except for one middle-aged man with a three o'clock shadow who sucked on a pacifier and goggled at Adam. Adam's remaining teeth bathed in blood. His face distorted with pain as if a spear pierced it. Things whirled in his head then went dark.

He is moving down a dark road, lost. It is quiet, still. He hears the faint sounds of bare feet behind him. The soft steps patter on, grow clear, and, close; then, come to an abrupt halt. He stops, scared. He turns to check his backside and sees a huge lion with white eyes sitting right by his side. Yikes! He walks on to see if the lion would go away. The lion walks with him. In the dark he does not see the hole till he places his feet out in emptiness and shoots down. He tumbles in blackness not seeing when or if he is going to hit bottom. "A long way down," he thinks; and then, everything goes blank. Before he knows it, he is deep in water. He tries to reach the surface but goes down further and farther. Submerged, he fights the instinct to take in a breath. But then, his mouth opens wide; water rushes into his windpipe; his voice box muscles constrict up and overcome his breathing reflex. And, just prior to suffocating to death, in a snap, he starts out of the blackout.

Adam sat with one unseeing eye as if far away. Noises and voices get louder and clearer till they float into his ears with a sis boom bah!

Guitars, cymbals, and pipes struck up. Drums banged out: *boom-boom–boom-boom*. "*Olé!*" someone flourished on a deft cha-cha move. A party had broken out. They were on a wide shelf on a foothill with a stage covered in canopy. Crowds hoarded under colourful awnings filled out stepped steps carved out of the hill on either side of a flat, sharp ramp. Wooden trolleys ascended descended to the left of the steps. A priest, a rabbi, and an imam stood stoic on the stage in formal dress. At the centre of the stage an arch two long ferns lean in to mark a great gate. Equidistant waterspouts spin from the sky. Streaks of rain scud by. A dreary, desolate landscape encloses the hill and the area. Adam and his backup were set on a sunken ledge to the left of the stage with no shelter.

The music stopped. A row of trumpeters stepped forward and blew a blast. The thick doors of the great gate divided in two and swung inward. À la a short pause, the tongue of the trump: Nacash Abaddon, tromps onto the stage. Dressed all in red: In a frock of linen sparkling gold. A showy sword tucked in a belt of silver all studded with gems. Donning a gaudy, rather pointy hat. He creeps to the edge of the stage; draws himself up; ogles Adam sidelong for a while, reflecting; then the tonguester holds forth as if annunciating a long-performed trumpery.

"Citizens of our One Kingdom! First, I would like to thank The Leader for his superb leadership." (Claps scatter.) Now! A great sinner has come before us. (A man blows a loud hoot; a few others join in.) He has confessed his sins. He has the mark of great Satan, himself! (*Tsk-tsk*, *tut-tut* clicks of disapprovals sound out.) And he is such a rogue and a daring escape artist that, even when chained and bloodied like this (he swings a hand at Adam), I fear that he could get away—at any time!" (A murmur disperses out.) Slack-jawed, Adam found himself gobsmacked by these colossal lies. Then, Nacash Abaddon, with flames dancing over his jet-black irises, segues to: "I now give you this carnivorous evil. Tie-stall of torturers. Silo-full of grass-fed lies. Butcher of abuse. The cruel, bloodthirsty god of hounding hounds!"

With that, a Black Helmet rolls Adam to the top of the ramp; then, tips the wheelchair frontwards. Adam hits the ramp head-first, flips, and ends up flat on his back.

(The crowd gasps.)

The Black Helmet picks Adam up by the pits and tries to balance him on his feet. Adam's legs give a few times from the enormous pain in his bones, but he does steady up on his shaky legs while coughing blood. Then the Black Helmet pushes him to go down the ramp. In silence, Adam starts shuffling on the steep slope, all bent over like he is in a Japanese bow, with his face locked up in hurt.

"Satan!" a woman yells out.

A man barks: "Sinner!"

The mob starts to heckle and gibe. A few lean over and spit. Showers of stones fly. He tries to dodge the stones to no avail. A man tramps out, holds and shakes a red cloth ahead of Adam. A woman shoves that man, then flashes and jiggles her big breasts. That distracts him, for a tick. But then a pile of hot shit hits him right in the mouth. He spits and snaps his head to try to get the feces out and off his mouth. At this point Adam starts to make a run for it; but he trips over the shackles at his feet, takes a tumble the rest of the way down the hill, and splats spread-eagled on a pavement. After a pause, a man at the foot of the hill in front of the crowd drops to the ground and doubles over in laughter. The mob busts out in howls, jeers, and cheer. Adam lay still; and, by some sort of a miracle, conscious, still. He no longer felt pain— though, his right leg, shattered at the knee, bent up in a cringe-inducing way.

A red van pulls up by in a screeching skid. Two men in red cloaks and helmets that have their glass tinted in featureless red hop out of the van, lean over Adam, pick him up, hand balm him to the back of the van, run around and jump in front of the van; then, with tires that spin out, smoke up, and spray gravel, zoom off.

The music strikes back up. A dozen hogtied boys are on the stage, strung up by a leg. The priest, the rabbi, and the imam pray over them. A tall, thick-set cutthroat—with a red face, in a green plastic apron, with a large carving knife—slits their throats; the boys thrash dangling—till their bodies drain out of blood. Next, several goons slice them up as holy halal and kosher cuts of meat.

~

It was night. The red van sped by a barbed wire fence with coiled razor wire on the top, gun towers, and sentries on patrol. The van stopped by a wide iron gate with "Newborn Prevention Centre" woven in on its top: and weaved in below the gate: "*quia in inferno nulla est redemptio*"—("because in Hell there's no redemption").

Searchlights that peered out to the dark backdrop spun and converged down on the van. From the crow's nests which flank the gate, machineguns redirected down at the van. Red Helmets appeared all around the van with their machineguns drawn up.

With a brief crackled buzz, the electric gate took on a slow roll. The van inched in, paused at a worn brick guardhouse, and a Red Helmet cleared the van through. The red van crept along a long, narrow passage hemmed in by chain linked fencing and curled razor wires; it then drove thru a large graveyard, around a long barn and a hexagonal shaped, heavily fortified building; and backed, beeping, to doors marked in red with INFIRMARY. A blond nurse swayed out with a stretcher. Red Helmets jumped out of the van, manhandled Adam out of it while he cursed them out and all who had brought him to this point of pain, restrained him on the stretcher, and rolled him into the hospital.

"All the bandages and plasters we have won't fix this one," the nurse mumbled under her breath.

Chapter Three

Newborn Prevention Centre

ADAM'S NOSTRILS flared up and stung from a thick, stifling stink: a mingled stench of urine, feces, undeodorized pits, and peppers. There were screams, moans, whispers, the sound of chains, and an electric hum. He felt concrete and woodchips beneath him; a tag stapled to his left earlobe and a loop ring pierced his nose. He opened his eyes. He was in a barn. He sat up and a chain around his neck tied to a horizontal rail jerked him back. He felt a chill. He was naked, in a six by three feet *tie stall*, enclosed by looped metal dividers. The base of the dividers had water bowls above a feed surface. Alleys split the stall rows, with gutters as for toilet. He scanned about and saw rows of bald, nude, pregnant women chained in stalls as far as the eye could make out. The emaciated women all lay or sat in fetal positions, trembling and, or rocking. Adam went to stand but a wire above him electrocuted him; he seized and toppled in a seizure. The barn's lights dimmed, then, drew back up with a strain. Red Helmets, gripping electric prods and pepper spray, ran all around about searching for the culprit.

The Red Helmets converged on Adam. One unlocked his neck chain. Another handcuffed him behind his back and gagged his mouth. A third hooked a leash onto the nose ring and pulled Adam down the long, lofty barn, out to the picturesque grounds of a dairy farm. Adam looked up at a poster on the barn with the image of a laughing blond woman and teenage girls in a field of green; with the slogan: HONEST ETHICAL DAIRY. WE CARE! WE KNOW EACH OF THEIR NAMES! Adam strove to breathe. Salty snot trailed his mouth. The Red Helmet drew him by the bone orchard a few paces from the barn to a white two-story house with a charming white picket fence and a white wrapround porch. Adam felt the stretched bite of the nose ring and feared it would rip right out. They went to the back of the house, down a few steps to its basement: a dim, low-pitched, stuffy cellar, with a sharp, sweet reek of rotten meat. The Red Helmet yanked Adam to a loadbearing pole at a corner of the cellar, knotted the tether to the pole such that Adam's nose just kissed it, and left. Adam could not budge an inch. He was in a fearful state. He felt—heard his heart's ta–thumps. A lanky man in a red cowboy hat that grazed the ceiling, cowboy boots, and a plaid shirt, appeared in front of Adam. He looked to be about fifty years old; with a red complexion, bushy brows and side-whiskers; lynx-like, scornful, blackened eyes; a thin mustachio twined to points across his sunken cheeks; thrust-out stomach; and a stretched out, dangling Adam's apple pouch.

"Been a-waiting a long, long while for this, boy," the man said in a raspy drawl.

As he spoke the man paced the mucky basement; and to see him, Adam, short-leashed to a pole and not able to slant his head, had to shift his pupils, back and forth, to the corners of their sockets.

"Been in a coma, you know—not a real one—*induced*, they say. Hauled fancy a-hole docs all the way up from the city to fix—

Devil take it!" He removed the gag out of Adam's mouth. Adam worked about his sore mouth and jaw; straining to not place too much pressure on the nose ring as he stood naked fettered to the pole by the nose with the neck chain down the centre of his chest.

"We need a lot of answers from you..." He produced a big file and ran a stump of a finger down its flyleaf. "Aha! Here it is! Aa..., dim..., ahh—is it?"

Adam did not respond; he had decided to keep his mouth shut. A shadow fell on his heart even before he opened his eyes in the barn and went down in the cellar and felt the man's presence and then saw him. His heart was troubled, and it struck him that that was not at all a nice place as soon as he had left the tie stall and saw the green grounds and that idyllic white house; it was as if wicked people had built the place.

"Been told you knew your name and that you talked right, right after you were born. Now, how's that doable, boy?"

"I don't know."

"You don't know? What kind of a name is that, anyways? Never heard of it," he twirled and chewed on his moustache.

"I don't know."

A spasm of anger came over the man's face. "I don't know, I don't know, I don't know! What do you mean by you don't know?" he demanded with a sharp, suspicious, annoyed tone. He got up in Adam's face, screwed up an eye, and stared awhile as if he were examining a thing he'd never seen. As the man fixated on him it was as though some thing penetrated Adam. After that, the brute jolted back; and, astride, with arms akimbo, wondered: "What's so special about you, anyways, eh? Where's the marvel, eh?" He tilted his head, leered over Adam's genitals, and a wolfish sneer raised on his lips. "We still have to give you your haircut..." He snorted out, slung his cowboy hat on a rack, and set out to work.

Adam gave all his mind to listening as the man stomped to and fro behind him.

Crash, boom, splash, hiss, sizzle, squeak, clang, buzz, click, crunch.

The ball gag swung under his chin and tied behind his head as he put up a fruitless fight. Ropes tied onto each ankle, pulled, and secured to hooks at the bottom of the corner walls. A bench was set; a jar filled with a blue liquid and fleshly balls; a scalpel; and an emasculator.

Adam moved his eyes the furthest to their corners to see the bench: its contents: and worked out what is a "haircut". Goose-bumps broke over his naked body. Adam begged and pleaded as best he could thru the gag to stop the man, sissling and frothing.

"Don't you fret, boy. My family's been in this line of work for generations. Plus, we have a big binder of guidelines for this," he said; and held up the emasculator (a plier with a straight blade and a round crushing clamp with jaws) and squeezed it for show; then, a white, bulky binder, titled "Ministry of Agriculture, Food, and Rural Affairs".

Fright took over Adam. He struggled to disengage himself from the pole: gathered all his will, and wrenched his head back, again and again, to rip the ring off his nose; fizzling snot bubbles.

"Boy! you're barkin' at a knot. Even if you do that, you're cuffed, and your legs are all tied up." (The man had a point.)

Adam bleated in a muffled tone. He sissed, gasped, sputtered, and rocked himself. The man brought a big car battery, all wired up and taped, and placed it between Adam's legs. Adam felt fingers spread out his butt cheeks; then, a probe forced in his anus: an intense pressure. Next, the man turned a switch on the probe. Adam screeched and almost stopped breathing and went stiff.

A fixed current passed thru Adam's spine and paralyzed his muscles. He was still conscious but not able to vocalize nor move. (Rich dairy farmers do not want to fork out a cent on anesthetics for surgical procedures; so, they concocted a cold-blooded hack coined as *electro-immobilization*.) Adam had a high heartbeat; his face, contorted scarily in pain, had seized in a hundred wrinkles.

The man wiped Adam's scrotum with iodine; then, pressed Adam's testicles up, pinched the bottom third of his scrotum and cut it off. (Adam's eyes grew bigger and bigger and bigger, and almost jumped out of his head.) Adam's testicles, covered with a thin white membrane, hung down off of cords with arteries and veins. The man cut and tore away the tough membrane from the testicles. (Adam felt a shriek come up inside of him, but, thru the gag, it let out as a long sigh—tears issued out of his eyes.) Next, with the emasculator, the man crushed and severed the testicles' cords, arteries, and veins. Adam's bloodied balls dropped to the floor of the cellar and rolled away. He passed out. Blood drip-drip-dripped down, then, streamed down between and over his legs. The man scorched the wounds with a flaming poker, thrice.

Adam felt himself shaken, and then he came back to that hellish paradise.

"We're not done yet boy!" he chewed on his moustache. Adam looked up with his eyes. Seeing this, the man said, "Don't bother praying to God, boy. He can't hear you. He's locked up in here, too!" With loathsome snorts, he brought a soiled handkerchief unto Adam's face and unwrapped it with bloody fingers. There were two balls in the hankie. There was a raging glowering fire in Adam's brown eyes which would have had the Devil step back.

"Okay, okay..." said the man in a sheepish volte-face.

He dropped Adam's balls in the blue jar of balls and closed its lid.

"You've your yellow tag. Now you need our herd's crest," he said; grabbed an industrial stapler and a black, triangular tag of the red dragon; groped Adam's right earlobe and stapled the tag with an "Easy-peasy". Adam squirmed from the sting of the puncture wounds. Then the man sauntered onto the back of the cellar, came back with a red-hot branding iron, and hard-pressed it on Adam's forehead. Flesh sizzled and steamed up in smoke. "I own you, now, my boy," he said with a snort. Adam wept in a sorry fashion. "And you can forget that asinine name of yours. From now, you're named—he flicked the yellow tag up—#6646."

A Red Helmet freed Adam from the pole, the handcuffs, and the gag; rolled Adam back to the barn in a red wheelbarrow; and locked his neck chain back on the tie rail. (They had given Adam a pile of fresh straw in his stall for bedding.)

"Farmer burns bad," muttered one of the tie-stall girls.

Adam took a long time to find a sleeping position that did not cause unbearable pain; and one that did not choke him with the chain round his neck. He finally settled on a fetal position on his left side with straws between his legs to split them up because it was as though his groin roasted above an open flame. His right ear was sore from the staples. And his branded forehead burned up from the blistered, swollen mark of the seven-headed dragon. He began to cry out so wretchedly that he moved all the women in the tie stall to tears. Then, at last, he passed to an uneasy sleep.

In the dead hours of the morning Adam came out of a deep sleep, to find the dairy farmer shaking him.

"Rise and shine, 6646. Breakfast time, boy."

Adam taxed to force himself up, manfully, to sit; husbanding his strength against what was bound to be some awful torture that was to come. In the other tie stalls the women were all on all fours with their hanging breasts hooked up to pumps with hoses in large glass jars which were filling up with breast milk. As the farmer milked the women, they masticated silage from the feed surfaces.

Adam could not recall the last time he had had anything to eat or drink. Then he noticed tiny puncture wounds on his arms and realized they had fed him intravenously while in the coma. Adam drank the water in his bowl with cupped hands. Then he tried the silage and spat it out in disgust. A Red Helmet watching him went to the farmer at the end of a row of stalls and then they came back to Adam's stall; and the farmer took a knee in front of him. "Why aren't you eating your breakfast, 6646?" Fuming with rage, Adam lobbed his hands at the farmer's throat, was yanked back by the neck chain that dug into his neck, stretched out his fingers, and roared, "I'LL KILL YOU! DASTARD—MOTHER—" "THE CHAIR! THE CHAIR!" the farmer hollered as he fell back on his arse.

Red Helmets unlocked Adam's neck chain and forced him on a metal chair and restrained his head and wrists to the chair. Then held Adam's head back, pinched his nose, squeezed his jaw, and forced his mouth to open. The farmer shoved the tear-shaped end of a plastic tube in Adam's mouth till it hit the back of his throat and he gagged. The farmer paused and felt Adam's throat for the placement of the tube's bulb. "See, there's a flap that covers the trachea; if not, this tube will go down the wrong hole and you'll choke to death. So, when I tell you to swallow, boy, *boy*! you best swallow." Frenetically, he thrust the tube down Adam's throat.

"Swallow! Swallow! Swallow! Now!"

Adam's throat and chest were in agony. With watering frantic eyes, he gulped in the tube as he wheezed and writhed in pain. At the other end of the force-feeding tube a Red Helmet held up a funnel filled with the silage; he opened its valve, and the silage set in motion thru the tube down Adam's stomach.

"This is how we feed calves that refuse to eat," the farmer said. "Well, you're a male calf—we don't do this for them—but you're our *pet* now; and we need to take a-lovin' care of you," he added, then yanked out the hose. Adam coughed and heaved as though they had choked him from the inside. (The dairy farmers' force-feedings in the guise of benevolence has a real sinister, true cause.)

"Don't you puke it up, boy; or we'll have to do this all over." As Adam swore at them the farmer instructed a Red Helmet to watch Adam to make sure he did not throw up the silage; and, if he did not, to "take him out back and start his halter breaking".

Just then, a woman in a stall close to Adam screamed at the top of her lungs. A baby's birth was at hand? Her rapid slide to childbirth seemed to have caught the farmer by surprise. He told a Red Helmet to rush and fetch a towel, washcloth, and a pail of water. She was on her back on her elbows. Her contractions got stronger, longer, and more frequent. Her breathing was guttural, painful; her chest heaved as though she could not get air. Not anesthetized, she felt a strong urge to push. The baby slid down the birth canal, and then, crowned. The farmer kept on yelling, "Bear down! Push..., push! Push hard!" She cried out in a shrill voice. The farmer held the baby's head as it came out turned to one side. With the next push, one, then, both shoulders came out. Then, the farmer raised the baby up to the mother's stomach and it slipped right out; it squalled. "My baby!" the mother called; her speech broken with gasps of emotion.

The farmer drew out his knife and cut off the umbilical cord. "It's a boy—a boy!" announced the dejected farmer with a woe-begone appearance.

From all sides, women watched with grim, branded faces. The farmer pulled the baby's head back and sliced the knife along his throat. Blood spurted up the farmer's hands, shirt, and face. The baby boy gurgled…blood.

The mother, leapt to a crouch aghast, shrieked with flashing eyes.

The whole barnful of women, till then silent, wailed as one. The dairy farmer glared madly with bloodshot eyes and a blood-stained face. Suddenly he drove his clenched knuckles onto the mother's head, driving his blood-spattered fist down on her with all his may, again and again. Compassion and hatred gripped at Adam's heart, at once, and made it throb, violently.

Shaken and distressed, Adam shouted, "You can't do this!"

The farmer rasped, "Sure can," as though he had a full right. He ordered the Red Helmets to batter the pregnant women in the tie stall with prods till they all gave him *girls*. As a rule, all of the women cowed to a fetal position, covered their heads with their hands, and beard the beating in womanly grit. (They seemed to expect what was taking place.) The uproar of prods striking their naked bodies was beyond the pale. The dairy farmer bellowed at the top of his voice, "Give her! Whack her! I want heifers. Heifers! Right here! Lay it on this one, hard! Harder! Heifers! Over there!" He ran up and down the rows of stalls holding the dead, bloody baby, dancing about the tie stalls in the most unseemly, indecent way. His red hair and moustache hung wet over his face. He was thrilled, amused, and cackled such a horrible laugh that it cut at Adam's heart. "Him! him!" roared the hideous, bloodied beast, pointing at Adam. "Zap him! Him! The girly boy... heifers—"

As a Red Helmet led Adam down and out of the barn, the sullen women held black eyes, red faces, and bodies bathed in blood, sweat, and welts; few glanced up mournfully. There was a faint jingling of chains, and the sounds of quiet, restrained sobs. The mother was beside herself. She kicked, bawled, and bawled; and a flood of blood gushed from her due to her placenta having had just broken. The Red Helmets rolled in the aisles in a muffled intone with no pangs of conscience nor shame.

It was a clammy dawn. The Red Helmet short-leashed Adam by the nose to a post of a chain-link fence at the back the barn, cuffed him behind his back, then left. Beams of two searchlights crisscrossed the grounds in front of him on the other side of the fence, casting shifty, elongated shadows of trees and the meshed fence. He could still hear the mother's heart-rendering cries. He heaved deep sighs from a full heart. He yearned to free the fettered souls from their suffering. He felt so, so sorry for them all; and thought heartache would torment him more than tortures and thrashings. Tears glistened his eyes. The way in which those stoical women had borne the beating had struck him. None had uttered a groan. Those women knew how to bear pain. Years of utter abuse had inured them to blows and plays a key in their fortitude, no doubt. The poor souls had grown used to their misfortune, to suffering.

The barn backed to a scorched forest. Looking thru the chain-link fence, the woods receded to a white mist; with squat trunks clad in a shadowy-black, gnarled and gaped, with stripped branches that reached out as bony, groping fingers. Adam gazed up at the strange, mysterious sky (so to speak), coloured a cool, pale steel. It was as dark out there at dawn as dusk. It seemed as though he was dreaming a dream: a nightmare, which led to no awakening.

There were no signs of living moving things. The place, the solitude, creepy trees: all appeared to be hanging on with bated breath. Everything was still; each sound seemed sharp and near: a door creaked, a branch cracked, chains clanged, a whisper: all gave him dread and fright. But not knowing what was about to happen to him next that scared him the most.

He shifted his pupils to the right and saw the fence and the barn vanishing to a point. He scanned left and saw the corner of the wraparound porch of the white house. The farmer was barbecuing. He looked to have showered and changed to clean jeans and a plaid shirt, slicked back hair, and a twirled mustachio. The headless skinned body of the baby boy hung by him with a missing leg. He sat on a white worn rocking chair and spied on Adam with a smug grin as he rocked, sipped and blew a steaming mug. After a while, he raised from the chair, closed the grill's lid, took a stride, stopped short, puffed his chest, then strode out of view.

By instinct Adam knew a base thing stood behind him and tensed up. "Shh..., easy there...," the farmer stepped to his side. Adam had wasted to bone: His belly had sunk. Ribs jut out. His hair and beard tousled. And covered all over his body in cuts and welts.

"Thirsty?" he craned his neck to Adam's face; then, took a bite off the seared baby leg. "Tell me how you knew your name and awake up there and you can get some Adam's ale and veal." He set eyes on Adam's fierce eye, turned heels, and left. Seconds later a door slammed, and the porch lights of the house went out.

(In truth, Adam did not know the answers to the questions. Like blanking out on a dream as soon as waking up, he did not recall much from before he woke up there. He just knew his name and that he had had a life on Earth—and a cat—yes! he *had* had a cat.)

Up to this point Adam had been dreading some awful thing other than tied to a pole. But then he recalled the farmer's words: *halter breaking*. It was then that he grasped tied to a pole as he was so that he could not move an inch was not meant as just physical torture, but it was to break him. (A trauma the East German Stasi coined as "decomposition".) He vowed not to give in. Adam was stubborn—he knew that too.

He felt done in by both in body and spirit, though. He ached to the bone. He braced his hands to take the stress off his cuffed wrists; turned his shoulders and ankles; and switched his weight on a foot, then the other. He stood the pricks between his legs.... All he knew was that he was in an agonizing pain for a long time; it may have been only a few hours or days for all he could tell in that sunless hellhole. It was as if he had awaked in a coffin and scratching to get out to no avail. How long could he bear being short leashed to that fence before giving up or going out of his mind?

He ought to take his mind off of his body, he thought: the body is the objective state of the mind. He fixed on summoning anything else from his past life on Earth. He fell into thinking and made a great effort to dredge up something out of his past. He turned and turned the dip in his mind as though dropping in on a far away sight. But Adam could not even draw out what his own face looks like. From time to time, he felt a dash about to come back to him; then it would all go misty, again. He almost burst his brain, but cracks at evoking the past were all in vain. He grumbled and cussed and chewed on what to do next. He set out to count the poles of the fence; he counted a hundred and two of them. He counted the trees he could see; he tallied two hundred and three trees. Then he added up branches, and then their twigs. He had the idea of splitting the infinitive as the way to pass time:

"I simply want to live. I want to simply live. I want to live simply. I want simply to live..."

He placed his head on the pole and pored over through the fence. With his eyes set, he peered deeper and deeper into the desolate expanse of the dead forest beyond that which met the eye. There was an affecting thing in that stark forest. He stared with a far away eye to the distance as though he made out some thing else. His absent-minded eye drew out a clear image in the veiled void. He had begun to dream of freedom and to scheming all the ways he could escape.

He supposed on a go at a leap over the hedge; where he may run to; and when he might do it; which bolstered his heart with yearned prospect. Adam mused and mused, and hope began to rouse in his heart. But then doubt crept into his dreams. Where could he go? What was beyond the forest? What was *in* it? What about his marked head? And what would be the consequences of a failed prison break? And the here and now cut in: Breakout was not possible. It will all be the same the next day as it is today, and the day after that, so on and so forth, ad infinitum. At this point the silage started to act so that he discharged with such a force his rear, legs, and the ground sprayed over; and he made a pool of blood.

Firm, rapid steps of a Red Helmet came up. He untied the lead off the fence, and led Adam to the barn, and past the farmer. The cowpoke, sporting his red cowboy hat, had an arm all up in the genitalia of a bare, chained in girl he forced to be on all fours.

"Suppertime! boy," he exclaimed with a turn of a gross grin.

"VILE RAPIST!" Adam castigated as he trailed by that scene.

As soon as his neck chain locked on the rail, Adam guzzled all the water in his bowel; and, like a slow-witted man who takes no time to chew, gorged the silage in front of him.

The women in the tie stalls rounded their backs and emptied their bowels in the gutters, here and there.

"Go and get a calf jacket," said the farmer to a Red Helmet. The farmer forced Adam's arms in a thin, quilted vest; adjusted and clipped its front straps; then dragged Adam to the fence with a guard that tailed them with a pointed machinegun. He secured the leash to a post and cuffed Adam's hands to it. "Was fixing to hose you down, but they're calling for a bit of drizzle: that'll wash you up." He snorted, gave Adam's rear a hard slap, and then left.

Despair had knocked Adam out cold. His head turned in topsy-turvy. He had lasted less than twelve hours tied to the fence; and now, he had to last till the next morning, at least. He shuddered with dread. He felt crushed, defeated, and broken. He was on the verge of tears. He strained to see the bright side: the farmer had tied the leash to that pole so that it had a foot and a half of slack.

Dusk thickened. Mist rose from the dead forest like steam. Wind blew a chill, grew swift, and hissed in the trees. A branch tapped and scraped a window. Stronger winds streamed in through and piled knuckled twigs up against the fence. The wind moaned and sighed; and, here and there, trunks and branches broke off. Rain spat in big drops. It went pitch-dark. There was a loud clap, then, a deluge of rain sheeted down.

Adam quaked from the bitter cold. That life was no life. He did not have to go along with it, he thought; he could quit. He did his best to convince himself that he truly was in some hellish dream. His teeth chattered. He squeezed his arms to his chest to try to stop its fierce tremor. His fingers and toes tingled; then, his arms, legs, and, his perception, all went numb. He saw the forest fade, his limbs vanish, and then his whole frame fell from sight.

When Adam's brain turned back on, he was on the ground and disoriented. His recall was that of standing while tied to the pole with nothing in tween; he did not know why or how he lay there. He felt his nose; the ring had ripped out of his nostrils' bridge. (Adam had hibernated, so to speak. Cold water had lowered his metabolic rate down to a crawl and that had caused him to black out; then, he had hung from his nose, for some time: and the loop ring had torn off. Then, his bony, wet hands had creeped out of the cuffs. And the icy rainwater had preserved his tissue as well.)

"This is my chance," he contemplated. "I'm too weak," said the other half of his mind. (His mind changed with each thought.) But, with freedom in view, his heart resolved to meet the danger. He stood up on his raw frame, gathered his wits: strength from weakness; and, on a spur of the moment, hashed out a flight plan. Every couple of minutes searchlights swept the ten feet of space flanked by the fence and the Dead Forest; strict watch kept from above checked it. Adam had to scale nine feet of fencing, go over coiled razor wires, come down, and run that field in that time.

It was the witching hour. The downpour had not lasted that long. The fence glistened with drops. Adam slipped one arm out of the calf vest, gripped the fence, and hung on. When the spotlights went by, he faltered, figured he had wasted time and had to wait for a fresh window. The next two minutes ticked by in a hundred and twenty seconds. He felt and heard his heart thump. He scaled the fence. At the top, he let the vest drop to his hand, swung it over the razor wires, squeezed his hands and arms thru the fence mesh, snatched the vest's buckles, drew in and clipped them back. He pulled up on the vest and flipped over the wires; just then, the vest's buckles came undone and, somehow or other, he landed on his feet on the other side of the fence. He ran to the Dead Forest, to an ominous mist that opened–closed before him.

It was quiet, and quite dark: pitch-black, in fact; Adam could hear and see nothing. He had planned to run that forest; now, he had to take small steps with his arms raised, palms out. Bare branches scraped his hands and slapped and scratched his face. He tripped over a log. He searched the forest floor and found a stick. He then walked with an arm stretched side to side and a stick that slashed here and there, scrambling thru roots, logs, and ruts full of water. Soon, the searchlights were like criss-crossing laser beams.

All along, Adam heard queer noises, and had an unsettling sense that eyes kept a close watch on him. And, step by step, the feeling grew—till he swung his stick to a side or the back as if the whatever-it-was was right *there*.

A bell tinkled by; at some distance, two great hooded red cloaks streamed in velvet darkness in a hollow cry and vanished. Adam crouched on a knee. A chill swept through him, and all his hair rose on end. In the dead silence he could hear his joints crack creak. There was a rustle in the blind dark above. A pair of bright, disembodied red points flashed down at him, and then switched off. Adam, rooted stiff to the spot with a gaped mouth, did not dare move as though he held out for a picture. He felt something creeping near and saw a deeper shade of dark in the black space. *'What's that?'* thought Adam, struck by terror. The blot got bigger and bigger, and near, but then it shrank and faded into blackness.

Adam had the heebie-jeebies. As he knelt, he got a hold of himself; then took on a slow crawl with searching hands. He felt braided roots and a big, knotted trunk with a wide slit. He leant against the tree with his knees up on his chest, clutching the stick; and listened in, for sneaky noises: for a step, a snap, a crunch, a bump, for hours; but he heard no sound, not a squeak. His eye lids grew heavy, his head dropped—he caught himself, and then he nodded off, again, and again.... He slept like the dead.

It was the crack of dawn. Drops fell from glistening branches and twigs that looked like they had had a coat of varnish. There came stifled echoes of barking, howls—"Hounds!" Adam rose. A huge tree with weaved roots and a cleft to a hollow heart leant over him with spread bare branches. The sounds of many thumped footsteps were coming up close, fast; as well as the shrill howls that rung out in the Dead Forest and distressed the heart. Adam stood and saw red lamps veiled in smoke swaying and blinking. They were near; so close they were about to reach him. He had to make a run for it. Mustering his strength, Adam sprung to a sprint. A pursuit was afoot. (Dashing the Dead Forest, helter-skelter, all blue and dried up like a wraith, Adam really did look like a spectre in an otherworld.)

Horn-calls and a ruckus of yaps rang out; they had sighted Adam. The hunting pack gathered steam and drove to a charge. Adam ran as fast as a fox—on his tippy toes—with hasty glances to his rear—fiery eyes were closing in on him. The burning of the nibble of muscle which he had left on his bones was not bearable. He could not outrun the huntsmen; and he had to come up with a plan, straightaway. He spotted and sprang into a deep gully, then took an abrupt turn and double backed to the big tree. The hounds hung back. Adam had given them the slip, so he thought. He got to the big tree, stole in his frame, and shrunk in its trunk. He heard grunts. He peeped thru the chink of the tree and saw a squat of a man all folded over in wrinkles; with droopy eyes and cheeks; a disproportionately small head and long ears; thick lips; bewhiskered; and, with a fleshy, red, moist, savagely inquisitive nose. Adam went stock-still, seized by fear. That creature of a man sniffed the forest on all fours closer and closer to the tree, mulling the scents; then lunged and raked unto the trunk with a feverish eye and quivering lips, and broke into ferocious squeals.

A pack of shrieking hideous beasts closed in on the tree from all sides. Wrinkled, hungry faces thronged their seeking arms in the cavity and pawed at Adam; he was in a tight place. With his body pressed up against the wall of the tree-trunk Adam sweated to shrink from all the long-nailed, bony hands. Their dogged doggedness managed to tug Adam out of the tree by the hair. They all fell on him, one on top of the other; and, like demented fiends, gnawed Adam's fluttering body; as he cried, they tore out lumps of flesh, hair, and beard, and the tags from his ears, and growled. A whip hissed and clapped. The voracious beings broke up with squeals and yelps. The whip whirled up, again, lashed out and curled about Adam's neck. A gleaming lamp hung from a beam thrust up on Adam's head. A curled moustache showed up in the light, and twitched, meaningfully; Adam saw it, at once, as the farmer's mustachio. He, in a tawdry hunting outfit (black knee-high boots, white tights, in a pink jacket, and a little black cap), frowned down at Adam as if he were a god and Adam a badger.

"Boys," he snorted in a gulp of phlegm, then chewed on his moustache. "String him up!" They tied Adam's legs and arms to a log and lugged him to the Newborn Prevention Centre.

The compound comprises a cemetery, a barn and farmhouse, and columns of domed, white hutches in which chained in girls come of age; acres of soy, oats, kale, barley, and corn: farmed crops that make up the silage (dubbed "grass"); and its grounds, where the hospital, Red Helmet's quarters, a sprawling hexagonal campus, and the warden's log house border a rectangular grass courtyard.

Adam was back at the hospital (a white low-rise building) and cuffed to a bedrail. A young, blond, blue-eyed nurse stitched his wounds while, now and then, slapped or punched him. Each time Adam went to gripe the nurse socked him an extra one. So,

Adam had come to keep his mouth shut and to take the hits while stumped. This was on top of the nurse not having given him local anaesthetics; so that each time she pierced Adam's flesh with the needle, he writhed and sighed, and, thus, got even more smacks. There was the hospital smell in there but mixed in with a sickly-sweet reek of rotting flesh. A stern, middle-aged doctor, with a bored, malicious gaze, was on his rounds with a couple of fair-haired, young nurses. They had thick German accents, blue eyes, and stub noses. They went to each patient and checked up on and probed him or her. "Soes zis hughrt?" queried the doctor as he twisted a man's thumb. "YES!" bawled the man. "Ant zis?" the doctor wondered as he bent and broke the man's thumb; the man blubbered in anguish. Adam, propped on his elbows, went to exclaim "What the—" but his nurse slapped his mouth shut. Adam pressed lips at her. "Zis man needz a cast," prescribed the doctor. They moved on, to Adam's bedside.

The doctor picked up Adam's chart from the bed's foot rail. "How's oughr new patient?" he wondered in an air of authority.

"Good," Adam's nurse drawled with a soft, mawkish voice. "Good, right?" she turned to Adam.

"Yes! good—Great!" Adam found himself professing to his own astonishment.

The doctor moved on. The nurse went back to her suturing work. Adam stared at her in puzzled eyes. She looked up at him; her blue eyes glinted and narrowed; the corner of her mouth and eye curled to wrinkle; but, in that instant, she slapped him, again, and turned away. Adam plopped down on and pushed his head in his pillow and puffed out. A smile flickered on the nurse's face.

~

Sentries paced up and down and guarded the door of that ward. (The hospital has two other wards which Adam did not see.) The heavy steps of the night watch came up to relieve the sentry on guard. The door opened, a Red Helmet stepped in and counted the patients. The door shut; the lights went out; and, with noisy clangs of guns and boots, the new sentinel commenced his duty.

Adam was not able to sleep due to the stinging, tender pains he felt from all over his body, and from the cacophony of snores. He lifted his head and regarded his sleeping wardmates. There were only a few in that ward. There was the man with the broken thumb across, an old woman with a hooked nose beside him, and some more patients whom he could not see in the dimly lit room.

Peals of crowing and chorusing sprung up in the corridor. The hearty roars got louder till there was an uproar by the door. Then, in rolled the doctor and the two nurses, screeching in high spirits. Their drunkenness had passed to a grotesque bwah-hah-hah. They were singing a form of *Es zittern die morschen Knochen* ("The rotten bones are Trembling") and making crazy gestures.

> *Denn heute, da gehört uns die ganze Welt,*
> *und morgen, und morgen, und morgen.*

The doctor stopped singing and, with a woozy finger to his nose, shushed the giggling nurses. "You vant painkilleghrs?" he yelled and scanned the whole ward in profound air of contempt. Adam browsed around and had went to put his hand up but the women next to him shook her head at him and mouthed *No*... The doctor went down the ward in unsteady, swaggering steps, and lurched and peeped in faces with a cold, blank, fixed stare. "Vant some?" he asked each patient. "Vant it?" A black man near the washroom responded with "Sure..."

Doctor Margue—that was the hatchet man's name—took out an axe and began to rain down blows on the man in heaved strokes. The man stopped his frantic screams after the third strike, but the doctor of death kept on chopping chop–chop. At last, he ended lamely and skimmed eagerly around with embers in his eyes. His hands, face, and clothes all showered in and dripped blood. His intoxicated bug-eyes gave way to a look of relief with a loutish howl. The nurses ran to him in hee-hee snigger. High spirits rose again; and they stammered out the door and down the corridor, singing: *Brüder, zur Sonne, zur Freiheit!* ("Brothers, to the Sun, to Freedom!")

Adam turned to the woman with a thank you in a whisper. "This here is dubbed the 'slaughterhouse ward'," she whispered back with a coarse voice. The night watch pitched the door open and warned, "No talking!"

On the spur of that ill moment Adam got the urge to use the washroom and asked the guard for permission. The Red Helmet uncuffed Adam from the bed and stalked him to the washroom. He had to step over a pool of blood, a hand, guts, and other gross body parts of the man hacked to death. The toilet lights flickered on and corpses with gouged out eyes piled in heaps struck Adam back. The Red Helmet pushed Adam back in and told him to go around the bodies. The sight and effluvia of the cadavers brought on nausea and fainting spells. Adam couldn't wait to clear out of there.

The next morning, hung-over Doctor Margue and the two nurses were late for the rounds. They got to Adam and the doctor asked how he was doing. "I'm wholly well," Adam declared.

"Put you just got heghre. Your vounds hafen't healt—"

"No, no! I've been completely healed," Adam insisted.

"I sink," Doctor Margue began then paused as if not quite sure. "I sink, you *aghre* healt," he said, and then scrawled something on Adam's chart. Whether the doc wasn't thinking straight, or for some other reason, Adam had got a lucky throw of the dice, he thought. And, in next to no time, Red Helmets transferred him to the main campus of the Center.

Barbed wires sealed off the six-sided campus from the rest of the compound; armed sentinels paced it; and sharpshooters holding long binoculars stooped on its roof. The first-floor common areas and the cells on second and third floors face in. At the core of the panopticon a brick silo goes up to its top with slots concealed by blinds and rings of floodlight to each floor: forming a sense of an all-seeing omnipresent eye (in a tower that could even be empty). Its first floor has six slices with each piece segregated for whites and the coloured: unisex showers, washrooms, and a salon, all in one section; a library; a school and a chapel; a mess hall; a solitary confinement unit; and an office area. The coloured folk dwell in the second-floor cells and the whites on its top floor.

Adam was handed a bundle of clothes (a set of blue smocks and white t-shirts, and a pair of black shoes) and toiletries; let to shower; then taken to the salon for a buzz cut and a shave. Adam felt like a new wraith. But he saw himself in mirrors for the first time and did not recognize his own face: all yellow, cadaverous-looking; with sunken cheeks and eyes with dark circles; a missing tooth; long, red lines of sutures; the swelled mark of the seven-headed dragon on his forehead; and, stitched nasal bridge and earlobes—not to mention his skeletal body: with long and short stitches, and red and purple welts. He was glad to see that he had been issued a black tuque: a knitted hat he could use to cover the mark of the dragon; afterwards, he had, always, worn that tuque.

Once he dressed, a guard escorted Adam to the warden's office. Inmates amassed around the silo; sat on benches or stood; talked or glanced up at tellies hung on all sides broadcasting a youthful, agitated Hitler; or were idle and wandered about. New prisoners turned out a buzz. The inmates gawked at Adam like how black men come to scrutiny in a white neighbourhood; indicated him with their eyes and exchanged whispers.

The clerical section is kerbed thru a long hall with thread-bare grey carpeting with red bands and spots and hemmed in by frosted glass and spaced out shut up doors. At the end of the strip there is one door facing out and marked with: THE WARDEN. A secretary's desk was on one side and a row of chairs on the other.

"Tell him to sit down," said the wooden, pale secretary with a nasal voice, blinking her green eyes at the guard as though she was just waking up. "Sit!" Adam sat on a chair and waited a long time, with the guard that stood stiff by him. The secretary's snug red dress swooshed like a pile of dead leaves when she stirred.

"Tell him he can go in," she slurred up, all of a sudden.

Put off by how the secretary looked past him, Adam did not wait for the relay of the despatch, went to walk in the office, but the guard stopped him short with a stretched-out arm. "Take off the cap," he ordered. Reluctantly, Adam yanked the tuque off his head and treaded in. Classical music played from a record player. A heavy-set man in a red cloak, with bulging red cheeks, an egg-shaped head of strands of brown hair, with little piggy eyes, and specs down a snub nose, sat at a big, cluttered desk. On his right there was a narrow window to a parking lot. On the left, plaques, certificates. Behind him, pictures of Mussolini and Stalin flanked portraits of a young-looking Hitler and a man in a red cloak with his face masked by concentric rings of flames. The warden, glued on papers, eyed up with such a scowled eye, and gritted his teeth.

The warden stared back down, threw a hand to chairs at the front of the big desk and imitated to take no more notice of Adam: who had the sense the warden had not spoken, as yet, *as if* engrossed in his papers, *pro forma*, as a bid to boost his stature with a bit of acting. Adam gazed at the kitschy Hitler art: portrayed standing, turned to a side, with an elbow on a handle and a fist at his waist; bearing the black armband of the red seven-headed dragon; with the canvas titled at its bottom with: *Ein Volk, Ein Reich, Ein Führer!* (One People, One Empire, One Leader!).

"Are you esteeming our dear Führer?" raised the warden in a husky lisp and with an effeminate mannerism.

"Ya, right!" scoffed Adam. "You mean Hitler's a leader in this world?" As he heard those words leave his mouth, he knew he'd made a foolish faux pas, and thought: Good God! What did you say? And that was just what the warden wanted.

"So, you know our Führer's name?" he asked, as he studied the back of a small, plump hand and its fingernails at a distance.

Adam hesitated; scratched the mark on his brow; blinked to the left; and then blinked to his right. "Think I must've heard the farmer, or, the doctor, say that name," Adam strained to claim.

The warden knitted his brow and shot Adam a doubtful eye from the top of his specs. "Is that so?" Adam looked down.

"Must be," Adam answered crossly, and looked straight up.

The warden took off his specs (which transmuted his look), wiped it with his gaped sleeves, and stared Adam down with his short-sighted eyes and grinded his teeth. "You are a wily chap—well, not much of a man, now! The farmer told on you—how you, just about, escaped. But I want *you* to tell us your story—without adding or taking away anything—the complete truth, son."

The whole truth would not do, Adam weighed. And he did not like the two-bit shot at his manliness (reminder of *that*), at all.

Adam crossed his legs. "Let's see. I woke up," he began, "up there," pointed. "Was spun down to a pool in a cave. Then, met a Nacash…Something—the Keeper." Re-crossed his legs. "And, since then, I've only known slaps, kicks, punches, and bites."

"And how did you come to wake up?"

"I have no idea,"

"And how did you know your name?"

"I just made it up," he said in an ad lib.

"Your story's such a strange, novel thing; don't think any-one would be so sharp that he could make up such a thing," said the warden, and resettled his nose with the spectacles. "I'm on to you, son—no matter the stories—I know what you're up to—no matter how you cover it," he insinuated and drew circles with a pudgy finger around Adam's head. Then pressed a button on an intercom on the desk, bent to it, and asked, "Is the party ready?"

"Everyone's ready," replied the secretary's crackling voice.

"I am telling you the truth," said Adam with a feeble voice.

"You're lying like a knave!" thundered the warden.

"Your suspicion's uncalled—"

"Enough!" the warden struck the table with his fists—stacks of papers tipped over—the record player's needle scratched up—and sprang to his feet, leant over the desk, red-faced, and cawed:

"You're a fraud! and, sooner or later, you'll be turned out!"

"I don't know what you're talking about. I don't know any-thing. Please, *please*, you *must* believe me," beseeched Adam in a pained tone.

The warden turned to the portraits behind him, pondering; then said: "We live in an evil world. I've learned to be forbearing, in coping with liars, frauds, outside agitators…" Then, turning, "I've lost my patience," he broke; shambled to the door, pulled it open, and vented, "Son…, it is time for your Red-carpet Soiree…"

Adam turned in the chair and looked back thru the door. On each side of the corridor stood a swath of Red Helmets, which held whips (made from tire strips). Two of them yanked Adam out of the chair and attempted to strip him as he wrangled with them.

"Warden! *Please* don't do this," Adam squealed in a fright. "My only sin's being born to this wretched—"

"Wait!" the warden charged the Red Helmets about to drag Adam down the hall. He came over on Adam, and aired, "You *were* born in sin—yes! that's true—and you can do nothing about *that*. But that's not why you're going to be punished."

"Why, then?" Adam twisted up appealing to the warden.

"For your refusal to confess to your sins, obviously."

"What *sins*?"

"*Exactly!*"

"What are you talking about?"

"Don't be cheeky, son. You think I like doing this? Do you think that I don't feel for you? Well, I don't—I mean, I *do*! But my hands are tied; cannot do otherwise; it's the law."

"What *law*?"

"The Lord's! certainly."

Adam dropped his head to the floor.

"Although..., the Lord God does tell us to be merciful..." Adam lifted his head and turned up in hope.

"But" the warden went on, "if I go easy on you, what will you and others think? That I've gone soft? That you can do what you want, and I'd let you off each time? I'd lose my authority.... Tell you what, son. If you run, some whips, no doubt, will miss, and it won't be so bad," he said with winks to the Red Helmets. Tears of fear ran down Adam's eyes. He struggled to free himself from the clutches of the Red Helmets. The warden told them to "Let him go," and then shouted, "Run! Son! Run! Go! Go! Go!"

Adam braced his head and ran down the hall. Whips whistled, struck him, and he got by half a dozen or so Red Helmets before he fell. The whips smacked his back back-to-back, one on top of the other, as he squirmed and screamed in agony and pleaded for mercy. Lash over lash his flesh burst open in a crisscross. The wet whips scattered blood streaks over in every direction: on the carpet, the frosted glass screens, the ceiling, and, of course, on the Red Helmets. Adam's yowls died down to moans; he ceased to thrash; then, went limp. Red Helmets pulled him, while his head and neck lolled on the floor, and chucked him in an isolation cell. The cell's thick door slammed with a foreboding, echoing *clang–click*.

Adam was in a six by ten feet cell of a low, vaulted, brick ceiling; with concrete stool and desk; a concrete slab with a thin, soiled foam for a bed; and a stainless-steel sink and toilet combo with a mirror on its top and a towel rack by it with a small white towel.

He lay still on his stomach on the cell's concrete floor with his eyes closed, for a long time. His back, torn up in stripes, had reduced to a flayed meat that oozed blood down his sides to the floor. When his eyes opened, he moaned in agony while rooted in spot, for a time; then, his eyes fluttered and shuttered again. Once he came around, his back, ripped and puffed, had steeped in blood and secretion. He had dried out to the point of delirium. His back burned, scorched. He strove to stand to carry himself to the sink but kept falling to the floor. Yet, with all this, he reached the sink; with a trembling hand turned it on; wet his parched lips; then skewed his head and gulped a profuse amount of water. He twisted his neck, glanced at his back in the mirror, and turned from sight of it. He took the white towel off the rack, soaked it in cold water, then gently draped it over the torn flesh of his back.

He shivered all over as if he were in a fever. The cold acted on the cuts and on his nerves and strained them beyond tolerance. Adam's face went pale, his eyes shined, and his lips trembled. He began to pace the tiny cell, from side to side, time after time. He was on edge, in a world his own, and looked about with a weird, wild eye. He rinsed the blood-soaked towel in cold water and placed it on his back, time and again. The cell's floor flecked with bloodied drops. At times, he mopped the cell floor with his ripped t-shirt. That night he keeled over in sickness; and then he drenched in so much sweat he thought his life was about to end. All he could think of was how he was not dead. He figured since he had died one time, he could not die a second time. But then he recalled the heaped corpses in the slaughterhouse ward. (He was good at not being dead—a step ahead of his corpse, at all times.) On his front even a slight shift brought on physical discomfort, and he would flinch and tense up. He was wrathful. He needed to exact revenge. All night long he wished bad things. He dreamt of all the ways in which he could avenge himself. He had murder on his mind. In his fancy he impaled, ripped off limbs, hung, and mowed down everyone with a machinegun. Then, the still-living Adam reproached himself for all his weeps and all his weakness. "I'll claim full amends for each kick, punch, slash, cut, and bite."

He is in a town of grey ruins of age-old houses, walls, and towers, with only a distant noise of barking-mad dogs. He hears a sound like the rustle of leaves at his back, turns, and the tail of a big red cloak streams to an alley. He runs to a tower and climbs its dusty steps to its top. He scans down and sees two hooded red cloaks tuck in the tower and hears a shower of whispers from the flight of steps. The murmur of ebb and flow of waves hails overhead. He turns up and sees great big foam-streaked waves crash above his head. How can there be a sea of waves up in the sky, Adam doubts. This is a dream: he is in a dream, flickers in his mind. He turns down the stairway and sees the great red cloaks just about reaching the top of the tower. There are no paths down off of the tower save by the flight of steps; no ways off it except by jumping over its face. A fearful confusion sets in. What is he going to do? He picks up his eye to the sky and affirms he must be dreaming. He reasons that if he is correct and jumps, nothing will happen to him—but if he is wrong! he'll die. He pivots and the red cloaks tower over him with their faces veiled in the black of their hoods. Now he does not have a choice. So, he jumps, arms flailing. The fall is heart-stopping fast; he shoots down. He thinks through it: that if he is in a dream, he should float down; and so, he does. The acceleration draws to a slow-motion. His point of view pulls back smooth out of his body. He sees himself land fleecily on his feet. And he woke up with a lurch.

There was a row of clangs and jingle of keys, and a metal food tray thrust through an aperture at the foot of the cell door. Adam roused, and with great effort forced himself off the bed; and, in yet more strain, scuffed his feet to the tray, picked it up, and sat at the desk to eat breakfast. On the tray there was a piece of bread and meat, diced potato, cereal and milk. He ate the bread, the dry cereal, and potatoes, but did not touch the suspect meat and milk. There was a hullabaloo, an uproar, like at a fairground, from the cell door. Adam peeked out two narrow bars of a window in the steel door. There was a bustle and crush at the common grounds. The inmates were falling in lines for a rollcall, pieced apart based on race and sex. They all wore smart, brown uniforms, with the women in short skirt. The head Red Helmet stood out front and marked a clipboard as the cellblock guards went down each row and called out the head counts in voices muffled by their helmets. Most of the women and men were old or middle aged; the young, beautiful or handsome. Along with the division by race, the mix up of women with men was surprising; it would have been unheard of in Earth prisons. Adam tried to guess the sort of people they all were from their looks and actions; they were either cross or merry. With a few exceptions, they were vain, and so sure of themselves—boastful; and quick to take offence. They pranced around with an air of haughtiness—even the old—with a slanted tuque, sassy gazes, and rude taunts. Others, silent, glared in hate. Adam's cell had the view of the school and chapel, the mess hall, and the communal areas. After the count, the inmates filed in the school; and they spent the next six hours on the school's wooden benches, with ten-minute breaks. They had to learn geography, chemistry, biology, math, and physics; and had to read and write German, Russian, Italian, English, and *Blot and Boden* (Blood and Soil) books. They sat on low pews with bent backs. Their tyrant teachers, raised over them at lecterns, called for full obedience. The rest of the time they were idle; swore at one another; fought; were drunks and, or high; played cards till late at night; and, had fleshly orgies beyond what is seemly—within their own races, mostly. And all the guards turned a blind eye to all this physical gratification—debauchery, greed, and gluttony (which was odd); even encouraged those baser natures (which was yet more odd). Adam had a sense the place was not at all a prison; and, given its name, more a preparatory school for its subjects, for some object.

Doors slammed shut in loud clunks. Steps echoed away. Lights bumped off in sequence. The light of the hall came in through the two narrow bars in the door and cast a series of columns on the facing wall. Adam stared at the pattern on the wall, for a time.

The lights flickered on in little clicks, one after another. Buzzers sounded. Doors thumped open. The warden clumped up with a dozen armed Red Helmets. "Tossin' cells," a woman yelled.

Red Helmets fan out. Beds turn up. Items toss over in and out of cells—harmless stuff. Then, in one cell, a guard found a drawing of a woman clad with the sun, with the moon under her feet, crowned in twelve stars, and travailing at birth.

"I want this turncoat's pals—all on this block—given the third degree!" barked the spitting-mad warden and lit the sketch on fire. He nodded to a guard that drew up his machinegun and, with a *click clack*, sprayed that cell with a deafening, metallic *rat-tat-tat* while the red glass of his shiny helmet flared up in muzzle flash.

(Loud came alarms that blared all about.)
The warden puffed off to Adam's cell, tailed by that Red Helmet. Adam backed from the door. The door opened. The uproar of the alarm, shouts, and banging from the other cells was over the top. The Warden ordered the Red Helmet to wait outside by the door. Then, barreled up on Adam: forcing Adam to step back, bump the foot of the bed, and plop down on it. The warden stood over him and panted in great hate; as if thinking, when am I going to kill *you*? He flopped on the bed: squeezing in Adam to its corner; placed a hand on Adam's head; and, with an eye over his specs and snaps of tongue, punctuated his lisped words with feely rubs of Adam's head and neck while Adam cringed and squirmed.

"What...should...we...do...with...you?"

"What did *I* do?" Adam griped, all in all bewildered.

(Outside of the cell Red Helmets beat up and hauled women and men across the door in a chorus of caterwauls.)

With a big surge and heave the warden rose and sat on the stool in front of Adam and brought his nose to Adam's face. His eyes flamed, his face glowed as by a fire within, and he breathed with difficulty. He began patting Adam's cheeks with a doughy, sweaty hand as he repeated a question with his low, hoarse voice.

"Are you the one?" (Tap.)

"The one what?"

"Are you the one?" (Tap.) Adam shook his head back.

"*The one what?*" This time he laid stress on each word.

"Are you the one?" (Tap.)

The warden would have gone on but had a terrible fit of cough, which lasted for some time, while he waved a hand.

(The alarms cut off with a sharp chirp.)

He cleared his throat, croakily, bent his head, and went on in a confidential half-whisper. "See, I am under a load to produce results. Else, the National Security Bureau will mark my name as being not resolute, or, enthused, and I'll end up in the cell right next to yours. No one's safe from prison or from the beggar's bag, you see. So, son, if you don't confess, freely, we'll have to torture you. And we have skilful torture methods: The German Chair— where they'll tie you to a metal chair that stretches till your ribs shatter. The Flying Carpet—where they'll tie you to two hinged boards and place you in a variety of L-shapes, which will break your spine. The Tire—where they will warp you in a tire so that your head and legs are on opposite sides as they lash the soles of your feet. The Ghost—where you will hang from cuffs behind your back for days as they beat you, which will saw off and break your wrists and shoulders. Now, son, you do *not* want to go thru all that—any of that—trust me. And I don't want to put you thru any of it—all of that. You're half dead, as if in the limbo, already." The warden looked for a nervous blink and Adam's dilating eyes betrayed that he had, indeed, startled and struck a nerve. "Now, you may be getting philosophical here; thinking, we may as well kill you, so that all this misery can end. After all, you've lost your balls, eh? It may be soothing, even—to think that way..." Adam listened in with keen interest; he was convinced: that that life was death. (The shouts and the bangs from the other cells continued.) "Is torture prudent?" the warden mulled as if debating with himself, bringing a pinky finger to his lips. "Why terrorize? Reduce people to skin and bones? It lends legal cover. Confessions keep up the puffery of vast plots hostile to the system; since we force people to fess up that they had played a part in a sedition and, or treason. It scares folks from joining up in the revolt. It's meant to silence. And it's meant to produce words of loyalty to the regime. But I'm doubtful of coerced confessions since with each torn out nail, you'll say yes to no matter what, eh. And that's why I have written your confession for you, to tell the higher-ups what they want to hear," he stopped, feeling himself; bent his torso to the door; and turned out and held up a piece of paper.

"That's blank paper!" Adam howled, bemused. The warden turned the paper, held it under and over his specs—with his little eyes darting shifty peeks at Adam—turning as white as the sheet.

"Well, that dope secretary must've messed the page break, so the signature line printed on a blank page," he said, hurrying and lisping. "No matter, you can sign it just the same," he added with a wave of indifference. Adam had a sneaking suspicion the warden was fond of putting on an act; bent on making a fool out of others—as the dull-witted do—he must think himself clever.

Adam moved with indignation. "You think I'm stupid, ha?"

"Not at all. On the contrary. I trust you are of first-class logic and reason and can see that I have been frank with you; and can work it out that you'll sign this confession, come what may."

"You want me to sign a confession I didn't give and haven't even seen?" posed Adam in perplexity with a raised brow.

"Well, I thought I'd brought it—but, now that I think of it— it's best that you don't see your full and wide-ranging confession. Since, if you do read it, you are bound to not sign it; then, you'll undergo sever torture; and then you'll sign anything, even blank papers. And since this is so—and it is—you may as well sign this whole confession of yours, now," he finished, and pointed to the paper in nonchalance as if it meant nothing. (All became hushed.)

The warden had thrown Adam in a perfect sweat. He could not refute the warden's logic, presumed trickery, and was beside himself. Each feature in his face was at work. He wrung his hands and shook his head like a man who did not want to be convinced.

"Well, you know your affairs," held the warden; braced his knees, stood up, and wheezed. "But perhaps you just need time to think things through to see matters in their true light." Adam looked up with his branded forehead seamed chock-a-block in wrinkles. "Tell you what, son. I'll send you back to the infirmary to have your back looked after as a sign of good faith. Then, when you're returned, I expect your decision," the warden concluded. He shuffled to the door. Put a finger to his head and appeared to be chewing over some parting remark. Then spun about at the door, and, with a good-humoured face, said, "You know... that nurse's taken a shine to you," and dropped his eyes in discretion.

"The nurse!" Adam gave an abrupt start. "What nurse?"

"Your nurse. Nurse Sinon. That old knockout that stitched you back together." Blood rushed to Adam's face, and he flushed all over. "Heard some things... *Something* about your eyes, she's said," he said with winks; and then, with that, spun out the door. Fantastic farce, Adam thought. He sat with his head in his hands, struck he was by the devilry. Nevertheless, the aside on the nurse had had an effect; he could not believe a word of it, but, flattered, he smiled.

~

On a slaughterhouse ward bed Adam strained to pay no mind to nurse Sinon's tête-à-tête with a guard. She let out sensual titters, smiled and beamed. Her well-fitted white uniform cleaved to her voluptuous body. Strands of flaxen hair dangled from under her cap. A pink blush tinted her plump cheeks and pouted lips. Her bright blue eyes with sable lashes had a mischievous rascal spark which Adam liked in women. She drawled in a soft, sweet voice. And when she paused her chit-chat with the guard to tend to one patient, she swayed her full figure in a smooth, noiseless gait like that of a cat. Before, Adam's hostile view had not acknowledged her beauty. Now he had to fight to keep his eyes off the curves of her breasts and her hips with her slight bend over patients' beds. (A few patients were there; not those that had been there before.) She spoke to the guard by the way, as her glance wandered back and forth to Adam. She must have noticed that he was quite shy and tried to avoid eye contact and she found that very amusing; since her eyes shifted to Adam, all the time, and the instant she caught his eye, he snapped away. He felt the strong allure of her; and when he gave in to her irresistible draw, she would, at once, beam victorious. So, vexed at being unable to ignore her glances, he moved his body so that a partition blocked sight of her. But, after moments, drawn by her force, he tilted his head to see if she was still aiming to outstare him; found her beautiful head turned eagerly awaiting his look; and, having caught him peeping, she cooed out a belly laugh; and went over, soundlessly, to his bed.

"Look who's back! You are second to none in misfortune," she called out in her sugary drawl with a radiant smile of delight. He dropped his eyes, blushed hot, and faint shivers ran over him.

"Can't seem to stay out of trouble, ha, Mr?"

"Can't make a jot of it," he said. She was dreadfully close to him: The warmth of her body … Her scent … Her heaving breast.

"Sit so I can see what I've to deal with," she ordered; so up he got. She moved to his back and removed his t-shirt. "My goodness! What did you do?" she cried out with affected gravity.

"What did *I* do?" he choked up in a great bewilderment.

"You must've said *something* for the warden do this to you."

Adam grew quite cross. "I didn't say *anything!*"

"Don't get pissy with me, Mr," she pushed up her sleeves.

"Adam,"

"What's that now?"

"My name's *Adam!*" he said with some heat.

"Now, now, there's no need to yell."

"I'm not yelling."

"Oh-oh, right! You're not—I am, yelling." She glided round the bed, and, for no good reason, gave Adam two loud slaps on the face. Light through barred windows cast striped shadows on her face. Adam clutched his cheeks in his hands with an "Ouch!".

"To think I've lived so long to get spoken to like this..." She was on the verge of a fit.

He picked up in a surprise. "So long? But you seem—how old—never mind."

Her face took on a sudden change; in an instant there was no trace left of her anger; and she considered Adam with pitying smirks. "One day it might *all* come *out* in the *wash*," she intimated with a meaning eye she wished to speak to him, on the sly; and sashayed to his back. With what came of the Watchman Adam could not be sure if she had given him an eye or he'd seen it in his mind's eye. But as she treated his cuts, she spoke in his ear in a stage whisper (in confidence, but that others could have caught her words). "Listen up," she drew up, "I am going to help you escape." Adam reacted with a raised brow and leaned back with an air of wonder and caught a queer gleam in her eyes and eyed her dubiously. She turned in and squinted into his face. "Don't look, stupid," she sighed; and then reared the back of a hand for a smack and he snapped ahead only just in time.

"Why would you help me?" he doubted in a slow, low voice with a slight turn of a head to a side.

"The more you refuse to talk, the more they'll torture you, 'til they kill you. And then—well—and then, that'll be that."

"Still doesn't explain why you want to get mixed in; or why I should trust you."

"There isn't time to explain all of it. And there are too many ears and eyes picking and prying. Let's just say, that: you don't have a choice; and that, I'm coming with you." Adam had had to summon all of his strength to not twist and gawk at her. His jaw dropped; he sat with his mouth agape.

"Now you know enough to go with," she added.
He needed to ask more questions; but the devil! what question?

"Why would *you* have to breakout?" (that was the question).

She replied in a weak, woeful tone. "I'm a prisoner here, too. They say you can grow used to whatever. Not me. Not to all this torture and stinking bodies...," she claimed, eyeing the bathroom.

"But you're a nurse; why don't you leave?"

"I'm enlisted. Like deserter soldiers I'd get a firing squad. I was fixing to leave; then I thought, 'Why not take him with me?'" Her reasons were, at the moment, sound, went through his mind.

"Look *Adam*," she went on, agitated. "I've gone thru *a lot* to set this up; which, for the most part, wasn't easy: time and place set; arrangements made; guards won over—which is easier said than done..." She was raring to go. "So, Adam, you must decide, now!" she pressed, and seized him by the shoulders from behind.

Adam's head dropped as he tried to work it out to see if it seemed right. He could not help ruminating on the question: "What if it's a setup?" He was quite unable to decide whether to not trust her or just go with it. Doubt came over him; something tugged at him to not go with her. His head was one whirl of hope and despair.

While he was pondering what to decide, she took his silence for consent. At length, she came round and faced him; and as she treated his shoulder wounds, she spoke again, softly. "I'm going to leave my purse here by your bed and will come back tonight to get it; after midnight."

"Wait!" His eyes popped in alarm. "We're going to do this *tonight*?"

"Shh! Hush!" she glared at him with shining eyes. "Yes! No time to waste. The warden might take you back tomorrow."

"He says he'd go easy on me if I sign a fake confession."

She bent an intent eye on him. "Don't you trust him, Adam. He's horrid because he has power. He lies. There's not a word of truth to his words. It's all a lie! And he's suspicious to the point of madness," she reflected with intense emotion. "But what am I saying. *I'm* mad—*mad*!" she spun away and stamped her feet on the floor in intentional impressiveness, as though beside herself. "Listen, listen," she turned back and bowed down to Adam's ear and said much, quickly, in an undertone. "I'll come back tonight at shift change with the excuse I left my purse and will bring you a guard's uniform and a key. Then I'll distract the guard I've been working on—"

"Which one?" he wondered in curiosity. "Which guard?"

"The night-watchman," she said, and cocked her eye to the door of the ward. "And once I get the guard's back turned to the door, I'll tap on the wall with my nails: and that'll be your signal to slip out the door and down the hall and out of the front door."

"You don't have nails!" (he had noticed her nails only then).

"I have some," she winced, and raised the back of a hand to his face. "See?" Thinking she was about to strike him he pulled back and hunched his shoulders with his eyes aflutter.

"Don't be such a baby. Sit up, straight... Now—"

"Wait!" he commanded in a muted voice.

"What is it, now?"

"What's the key for, the front door?"

"No, that door's always left open. The key is for the gate in the fence. Once you exit turn left and walk straight till you come to the gate. Walk—don't run. Remember, you will be wearing a guard outfit; and, as far as anyone knows, you're a guard, on a break, out for a smoke. The only thing that you won't have is a machinegun since they keep all the guns in a room I can't get to. Once you're on the other side fling the key back under the fence."

"Then what?"

"Then walk, casually, to the forest; and follow the path—"

"The forest! Oh no! No! I can not go back in there," he shook his head.

"Why not?"

"There's something in there," he whispered, appealingly.

"What—what's in there?" she inquired with a grave face.

"Don't know. Some things, big, in great hooded red cloaks."

"Oh, that's just a run-of-the-mill old wives' tale," she said with a wave of a hand.

"What's an old—"

"Folks claim they've seen things in forests; they imagine it."

"*I saw them*! Wasn't my imagination...," he brooded. "What do they say they—those things, are, anyways?"

"Children call them Red Dragons."

"*Dragons!*"

He had the notion she was gazing straight past him. A look of alarm swept her face. Doctor Margue eyed them, watchfully, like he had heard all that had passed between Sinon and Adam.

"I'll meet you on the other side of the forest. Have to go—"

"What's in that forest?" he harried to ask.

"Whatever you fancy is there, don't turn back—and follow the footpath—that trail is the only way out of the forest," she told; studied him with a searching look; dropped her head; squeezed his hands in an awkward manner; and, without raising her head, turned as though she had to tear herself away—hands parted in a slow graze of fingers—and she rushed out of the ward in a great haste.

Adam mechanically sank back in the bed and his face contracted with pain. He stared blankly at a barred window: at a bleak, overcast sky, so to speak. A flash threw wild, grilled shadows in the ward. The lights pulsated out. Distant roars rumbled. With the next lightnings flareup, Adam saw no one in the room; as though he had turned his head and all the actors had exited the stage, en masse.

Chapter Four

A Shoeshine-boy Named Sergeant

ADAM CRACKED a head to the door of the ward as it swung shut. He had heard the thump-thump of flying steps of two, possibly, three figures who had, just, left the ward; none of whom had, on the way, said a word. There were soft plop sounds; a leaky faucet disturbed the still surface of a clogged sink. Light came thru gaps in the frame of the bathroom door and made the ward's darkness visible; and the sharp reeks of the decomposing bodies burnt his nose. The room felt overheated; sweat ran from his head. He took a look up and down the vacant ward; then, quiet as quiet, sidled the creaky bed—its noise boosted by the dead silence; as though by design, a complete stillness—and, scratching himself, scanned the room. Rain began to lash and stream the barred windows. He had not noticed a great deal while plotting with nurse Sinon. He had had no notion of the things that had gone on right under his nose. He saw trails of blood issuing from six of the beds occupied by patients before converging on and going under the washroom door.

Rapid steps thudded up the hall. Guns and boots clanged against the floor. The night watch had begun. Fixed on the door, a look of resolve came over Adam's face. He saw Sinon's head. He started, leapt up, then sat back down. His heart pounded in excitement. The door swung out, and she glided in.

"Just going to see if I left it here," she drawled.

The lights flicked on. She wore a well-fitted, dark-coloured dress, and held a knapsack. He laid back with an inward pang and clasped his fingers over his chest: to seem composed. For a moment she halted at a distance from him. He lifted his head to her and smiled. A curious change had come on her face: present, yet, distant. She pulled a face. His smile faded. With an abrupt animation she feigned a frenzied search for her purse as she looked to avoid Adam's eye and kept a sharp lookout for the door whence the guard's red helmet had, only just, protruded.

When she reached Adam's bed, she stooped, took a bulging bag out of her backpack and shoved it under his bed; stood, held up her purse, and declared, "Found it!"

Adam, half reclined on the bed, bowed to the edge of the bed, and mouthed "*This is happening.*"

With side glances, she scanned him, the door, then ducked out. He felt in his bones some danger hid from him. His intense wish for freedom had fogged up his reckoning, perhaps. Earlier, while he waited, he had thought: if he were a felon, then, he was going to be one; he had made up his mind to do what it took to escape. So, his doubt lay—but with doubt. He got up, retrieved the bag, and clothed himself in the Red Helmet get up. While he waited for Sinon's signal, Adam could only just hold himself back. His heart was all a pitter-patter. He heard sounds like tapping and scraping. *Tip-tap, squeak, squeak. Tip-tap, squeak, squeak.* The signal!

With one foot pointed forward and the other backwards, he hesitated; he shifted from one foot to the other; took off the black tuque; and then squeezed on a red helmet on his bald head. His eyes dilated as he saw that the helmet's red visor is a nifty heads-up display; with green lines and code: blinking his vital signs on the left and a three-D map to the right of its red glass. His brown eyes shined with red and green light. Through the red tint of the visor, he could see clearly, as if the light of the sun shone in the ward. He turned his head, spread his arms, and spun evangelist-style.

Tap-tap, squeak. Tap-tap, squeak, squeak.

Adam turned sharp, drew his arms back, and then, timidly, moved toward the door of the ward with little steps. Once he got to the door, he listened for a bit; snuck peeps out of its window; and, seeing and hearing nothing, he opened the door. In the hall to the right of the door nurse Sinon was making out with a broad, sturdily built night guard. Blocked up short, Adam impulsively pulled back, instinctively crouched on a knee, and struck stiff. He breathed by a hair's breadth. His heart raced in a swishing poum-poum. As she kissed the guard and clasped the back of his head with a hand, she glared at Adam with a wide-opened eye, briefly; then beckoned him to go with her other hand. Adam bowed and crept left in the hall, taking note of his light-footed steps at each step. Once he reached the front door, he looked back—Sinon held the guard's head with both hands, with an eye fixed on Adam—pulled the door and hastily turned out. But as soon as he stepped out of the door, he found a company of Red Helmets standing before him. This was unexpected. If he was surprised, the Red Helmets were more surprised still. At once, the door closed, and Adam gasped. There was a coming and a going out there, and helmeted and non-helmeted Red Helmets were thick at the door.

Lazily, they had all turned in to him and hushed up. Adam had frozen at the doorway as though a statue chiselled in mid-stride. With as much composure as he could muster, he chipped in their ranks and made for the fence. He could barely breathe.

"Halt!" a voice called out like a clap.

Adam pulled up short. A hand slapped him on the back of a shoulder. A short, thick-set, red-faced Red Helmet with a sharp nose and thin, dishevelled brown hair stepped in front of him.

"Where are you going?" he asked in high voice and peered in suspicion in Adam's visor. CAPITAN was on his smock's breast.

Words stuck in Adam's throat. He thrust his hands into his smock's pockets; and in one pocket he felt his tuque and a packet of some sort and in the other he felt something else. In confusion, he brought out his hands and found a lighter in one and a pack of smokes in the other. The man squinted at Adam's visor with a terrible, fixed stare, for what seemed a long time; then broke to a genial laugh. "I'm messing with you. Enjoy your break," he said, turning. Adam's all puffed up chest deflated in a long sigh of let off as he bent a courteous head to the man.

"Wait!" a Red Helmet yelled and signed to Adam to hold. "Who's guarding the ward?" He looked in the ward's front door window; and then whistled in and made out with some catcalls. Others came up in a pack, jostled and shoved in turn, to get a see. Adam broke off to the fence. When he reached the gate, he saw it padlocked, and recalled, "The key!" Scared stiff he had left it, he padded himself in all places, and found it in the smock's breast pocket. He put the key in the lock's keyhole, it turned, and snap! the lock opened. Once on the other side of the gate, he checked if no one looked at him, and found that the Red Helmets eyed him again. He relocked the lock back and headed for the Dead Forest veiled in mist. Trees that leaned in formed an arched entry to the

Dead Forest path. The visor's map showed the track as a squiggly red line. Stepping into the dim forest, he felt a heavy threat in the air. The rutted path had filled in with water. With the helmet the forest was clear and far seen, not like the last time. To make way, trees, broken and chopped, and rocks lay to a side. Rain specked the helmet's visor that fogged on up; so that, often, he had to take the helmet off to wipe its visor. Fog wisped like smoke. He had the tense sense, again; of some thing watching him, and waiting. There was a tinkling of a small bell. Behind him, a shrill cry rang out; then a fell cry replied back. Piercing chills went thru his back. He donned on the helmet as quick as thinking and scanned back. Far behind, the entrance to the stringlike trail was now like a pale tear. There, two red orange cloaked forms rose from the ground. Jeepers creepers! Draped in great big cloaks, the shapes bent and crawled into the Dead Forest toward him; and advanced swiftly, with their great red-orange cloaks streaming behind them. Adam knew that he must run for it; but as soon as he turned to—lo! he found himself sandwiched in between the two hideous, terrible forms that straightened up, jerkily, to tower him. The visor made their gruesome faces covered in hoods sharp and clear-cut. Short their mask of skin peeled to bone, pulsing pink muscles, tendons, and violet veins oozed gore. One gnashed thru tooth like a saw; and the other hissed out. All about the three of them loud peals clapped; then, a thundershower fell. The skinned faces of the Red Dragons spasmed in wrath, with red-hot coal eyes fleshed out of their heads that grossed him out. Horror-struck, he stood numb with his eyes and mouth wide, gaping up at them in shock. The brief shower came to a sudden stop. Something cracked. The Red Dragons twitched to it. Catty-corner to the track there sounded a bell. Jolting, they eyeballed a thing visible only to them. At that same time, Adam saw his chance, and stole unseen to the woods.

Charred, wet trees and branches were reluctant to let Adam through. There were drawn-out cries and wails that rose and fell. Shivers ran down his back. He broke to a run, leaping like a goat; fog wreathing about him. Once more, the visor fogged up; Adam did not see a log, tripped over it headfirst, splat! into a trunk, and kaboom! the helmet smashed up to pieces. Wobbly and stupefied from the blow, he could not call to mind why he was there; till he heard howls about the dark spaces, and all came rushing back to him. Night drew on and quiet. The sky, so to speak, was clearing. All around there, the night air hung black, thick and hollow. He waved a hand in front of his eyes and could not see it. Left with no vision Adam found his sense of hearing and smell honed. The damp woods smelled musty. A single near and clear bell jingled. Other than sight and scent, there was another sense, too; he felt a presence. He saw two red, glossy points that switched on off. The red pair appeared, faded, and blinked from different spots; then stared unwinking from a tree close by; all the while accompanied by the eerie sound of a bell ringing, soft steps, and scratching. He seized with terror, agape, with such killing look of fright—if one could see him. As he watched, the velvety black thing leapt off the tree across the dark space and crept towards him. The what-ever-it-was was a deeper shade of dark in the jet-black blot that lay dense all round it. Adam shook back from affright. And as he cowered to the ground, he heard the utmost surprising sound: a cat's "Meow!" Well, that was just the cat's pyjamas. The swish of the cat's tail stirred the night air and sounded noisy in the quiet. "Hey, you. What are you doing over here?" Adam whispered to the cat. The cat swished tail and said nothing. "So, that was you, ha?" "Meow," said the cat. A shower of whispers came from afar. He was about to ask the cat—but behold—the cat was no longer there; she had moved on. Staying still, he listened in to the dead stillness. Something crackled. Adam squinted forward and saw the cat at a way from him as a pit against the black backdrop. He homed in on and went to her, dodging branches and tree trunks. The cat moved ahead, and he shadowed her like a tail, guessing she was leading him. The quiet was so deep steps and splitting branches fell as loud scrunch, snap, and pop. The cat threaded in a winding way clear of the pathway, which was like treading on and on a round-about—so he hoped. They snaked a thin catwalk on the edge of a bluff—if Adam could have seen... His advance was slow for he had to fight thru dense wood of stripped trees, rocks, and rotting logs. He felt a cool early morning chill. Dawn rose as a pale silver light of a full moon. Twilit, Adam could now see the cat: black, with lamp-like blue eyes that glowed red when she turned back. At times, she would stop and wait for him with half-closed eyes while she watched him. The cat had, stealthily, wound the way to a levelled ground by the trail. They rounded a corner and were back on the forest track that ran like a tunnel to an open space. The cat looked at him mournfully. He shook from an ill sense. High-pitched wails fell down the path. He turned. There the Red Dragons were, again, a mile away, with their eyes aflame in the half darkness. Just then, several things took place: The cat vanished with a ding. The Red Dragons swept the ground like whirligig blobs of blood. Adam let out a yelp, sprang head-long, and made for the end of the track that lay just ahead. Like a galloping wind, the Red Dragons were at his back like a wart on a nose. He ran swifter. Any second, he felt, they will take him down. He cried, beyond winded, as he pushed on. The ground fell and, all at once, he was at the end of the forest in the open. He saw a road, a black car parked ahead, then a drainage ditch. Right behind him, the Red Dragons hissed with roadkill snorts. From the car's window Sinon beckoned him with panicked eyes.

Adam gathered himself for a leap, leapt the ditch in a long jump, and rammed the car. He twisted around just as the Red Dragons knocked into the car—clunk—clunk. He dashed to the other side of the car. The Red Dragons jerked up to giant red cloaks. Sinon squeaked and locked the doors. "OPEN THE DOOR!" he pulled the door handle; and kept yanking it so the door kept locking. "STOP PULLING!" He flung his hands and looked up. The Red Dragons shrieked with wide, hollow mouths; then, crawled to him over the roof of the car. He opened the door, jumped in, slammed the door, and yelled, "Quick! Quick! Go! Go! Go!" Sinon floored the gas petal and the car lurched to a start. The Red Dragons slipped off and rolled. Adam, clinging to the bar, beside himself, let out a hoot, in haste. Sinon, in the thrill of it, cut a couple of capers in the air with her hand, and beamed. Adam's heart pounded, and he could barely breathe; he wheezed with each gasp.

"See…," he said in a broken voice and pointed back with a thumb. "Told you they weren't old wives' tales."

She glanced at the rear-view mirror, then at him, with her eyes fixed to a squint; and then a cold look came over her face. "They weren't supposed to be in there," she said.

The Red Dragons, twitched in balls, rolled like an express train to the car, and grew larger and more red.

"Well, they're real. As you can see." He turned in his seat and looked back. "Go faster," he said in alarm, in seeing that that the Red Dragons were gaining on them.

She lifted her eyes to the mirror. "I know…," she said, and stepped on the gas. The Red Dragons fell back like red spots in a distance. She scanned him as though thoroughly perplexed: first, his head, then, his soiled smock caked in mud. "What took you so long?" she probed. "Where's your helmet? And why are you so dirty?"

In wonder, he turned a long, wild look on her; then, at last, controlled himself with difficulty and said: "You just saw them!"

"Should've taken you just an hour to cross," she claimed, and glared at him in defiance. "Been waiting here all night."

He fixed a piercing gaze on her. Then, curtly, with a note of fury, he said: "Well, I'm sorry. I had to dodge *dragons*! Hit a tree; smashed the helmet; couldn't see; and if it weren't for the cat that led—"

"Wait—what? A what–what led you?"

"A cat,"

"A *cat*?"

"Yes; a cat."

"What's that?"

"What do you mean what's that? A cat: a cat is a cat."

"You're making no sense. But go on..." she said, flippant.

He stared open-eyed at her. His face contorted. Then shook his head; took the tuque from the smock pocket and yanked it on his marked head; turned away and lolled back in his seat.

She skimmed him intently, for a time; and then said, "What? Not going to talk to me anymore?" Adam seemed to refrain from speaking, on purpose; turned up his nose, and said nothing. He looked out of the side window with glazed eyes. He felt weighed, faint. His eyes were closing from fatigue. "Got your freedom. Do I even get a thank you?" she scoffed. A light dawned on his face. Vexed with himself, he lifted his head to her shamefaced. "No, I'm sorry. Thank you." She looked at him with caressing eyes. "We're not out of the woods, yet" she said, and rubbed his knee. "We still got a long way to go." She pointed past his face. "Where we're going." Far flung, over shoulder-to-shoulder green hills, a black mass of structures hung in a haze. "You look beat. Should get some rest," Nurse Sinon ordered.

Adam, stretched out in his seat, looked out with half an eye open. They steered a circuitous string of road that looped in hairpin curves round and round and up and down undulating, lush hills. A fog-white sea of mist hovered the hillsides and hid steep falls. And as he sat reclined, Adam gave in to the spell of the deep realm of sleep.

~

He feels a lumpy pillow. He is on a creaky bed with a garish cover stained with a lot of round spots. He is in a small hotel room with a blistered beige ceiling. He is hot; sweat drips down his face. A fan moves back and forth on a rickety nightstand by the bed. A wicker chair and desk sit in front beneath a cheap frame of a pink flamingo. Wallpaper of a red flower peeled in swaths sheens in sweat and sags. He hears car horns; street traffic; muffled cry and laughter; door slams; distant phone rings; a woman's moans; the *squeak, squeak, squeak* of bedsprings; the *clack, clack, clack* of a typewriter; steps in the hall; and two quick knocks at his door. He gets up, opens the door, and cocks his head to each side of the long hall; it has the same torn wallpaper and a red rug. A row of red wall lamps blink. Sinon is in front of the elevator. She turns to him with a smile and waves for him to follow with a sly wink. He turns in to put his shoes on but cannot find them in the room. He walks out shoeless and sees her turn a corner. He goes to her. The wallpaper in the hall starts to glisten and droop. He is perspiring a great deal; sweat pours down his face. He gets so hot he wants to crawl out of his body. There is a hiss sound. Flames lick up the walls and bulge black smoke. Ablaze, the hellish hallway moans and sizzles all round him. He starts to run for it. There is a loud explosion that throws him, and he jolts up in the car seat.

"Bad dream?"

"Don't know..." He pulled up and tried to recall the dream. "I remember—" (he closed his eyes) "—nothing!" He had at once forgot the dream.

"We're here," she nodded out. There was a smell of smoke. They were on a steel bridge to a city of burned skyscrapers. The bridge was one mess of rusting steel beams and cables on posts thrust in a river that rippled and swirled about the pilings. Grass and weeds grew out of its niches. At its end, she stopped the car.

"Here; put these on." From the back seat she brought a pair of black pants and black hoodie and brown climbing boots. She popped the trunk and got out. "Be right back," she said. As he was changing, she walked by the car with a green army bag. She then ducked under the bridge. In short time, she came back out in black pants and black hoodie and brown climbing boots and no bag. She drew her hair in a bun and pushed her sleeves up.

Once she got in the car, she saw that he eyed her with prying eyes, and said: "Stashed guns."

"Guns!" Adam's eyes opened. "What for?"

"The plan is to meet up with the Underground. If they catch us with guns, they'll take them, or, kill us."

"Who are they?"

"The ones that still resist."

"How are we going to meet up with them?"

"Um..., we're going to find them?"

"How are we going to find them?"

"You leave that to me," she bit back. Then put in, "You ask too many dumb questions; did you know that?" and drove off. With an injured face he sighed and bowed his head.

"Going to use you to get to them."

"*Me*?" he perked up in surprise.

"Yes; they say you're 'The One'," she said with air quotes.

"Why do people keep saying that?" he asked, at a loss.

"Who keeps saying it? Who said that to you?" she snapped.

"The Warden. When he questioned me. He kept asking me if I was the one."

"What did you tell him?"

"Nothing. I didn't know what he was going on about. Do you know what they're all talking about?" he asked like a child.

She gawped at him, amazed. "You mean you don't know?"

"How should I know?" he said with a pained face.

"I don't know; you tell me..."

With those words they fell to silent thought. They had had struck a road long forsaken. Its asphalt had split and heaved up; shrubs and roots had come out of it. Leaf and grime heaped up. On each side, half buried in dense trees in swamp, lay car parts, a sink, a pan with cracked handle. They drove by a city limit sign nicked and poked in holes; with a big "BEËLZĔBŪB" scratched in over the name of the city. The patina had worn on a bronze statue of a nude man with two drawn swords. It was a city shot up and cratered to bits. Looted shops had their guts spilt out. Fires leapt like tongues. Tall structures had toppled and smashed in; with their steel columns that gnarled and buckled; some leant on each other for a prop: they groaned. Windows had blown and broken by bombs and the stress of the slumped walls. Pipes burst. Bricks crushed with mortars that crumpled like crust. A concrete jungle it was. Creepers, ivy, and vine clawed and snaked up walls and stained pipes. In it all were: rusted cars; torn tires; broken, pitted tiles; burnt up insulation; shattered glass; and curled up photos.

"What happened here?"

"War. Inflation. Famine."

"What war?

"World War... You know nothing, *Adam*," she teased.

"How would I know?" he griped, baffled.

"Forgot! you were born yesterday," she snorted. He smiled; and the smile remained on his face for a long time as if forgotten.

Aside from the plant life, there were no signs of life seen. Block after block, it was all a blank, hushed slate. But there was one man with a white beard, in ragged clothes and shoes, who talked to himself with a hand that moved in circles. Then they drove past a woman with a round face in a bright scarf and a grubby apron. These were people that eked out at the edges of a ghost city.

They came up to a bar with dingy red brick. "Sub Rosa" was on a worn sign above its stained, split door. Drunk men came out of it, staggered, and cursed and broke in song. On the other side of the street there was a black boy of about eight shining shoes. The boy kept an intent eye on the bar. Sinon turned the car to a dark alley at the back of the bar, and parked; no other cars were there. "Our best chance of finding them is here," she said.

It was a small, pitched room with an arched window; half veiled in smoke, with a heavy, rank smell, and lit by candles on lamps hung from black beams. Its floor's dark, rotting, marked planks creaked. A man sat at each end of the bar and behind it stood the barkeep. One man was a shaggy drunk that gawked in a creased tan suit; "Whoop-de-doo!" he said to the other man; saw Sinon and rubbernecked a "Va-va-voom!" The other man was a grey-headed man in patched clothes that sat as though pondering on his misspent life. Sinon and Adam sat at the rear of the bar on ash, gluey, notched table and chairs. The thin bald barkeep, with thick black brows, wore greased white apron, shirt, and pants. "What'll it be, then, folks?" he hollered from the back of the bar.

"Do you have beer?" Sinon asked.

The three men seemed to look them down with contempt.

"Just got moonshine up here, hon."

"O, all right—and don't call me hon. And tell that drunkard there to keep his eyes off else I'll rip 'em out," she scowled like a basilisk. All the men stirred and eyed one another and the walls. The walls, black on top from smoke, grimed glossy on the bottom from years of friction.

The bald man set the drinks on the table with a "Where you folks from?" His oily head flashed in the candlelight. Sinon's face went dark, pale. She exchanged an eye with Adam. "Where you folks headed then?" She looked up at the barkeep; they regarded each other for a wink. And then they all shifted an askance eye. Adam went to talk but she gave him a swift kick under the table to shut him; then he looked down at his clasped veined hands; and forced himself to keep staring at them.

"We're looking for our friends," she said in a cool manner. "Maybe they've been here?"

"Armies been through four—five times. Bar some knuckleheads," he swung an eye to the bar sans his head, "no one comes here, no more."

Adam, from under his brow, peeped up round. Tan suit, lit, drank his glass with relish and leered. The one with the patched clothe fixed as though keen to take a part in the exchange. "Red ranks come here," he said, cheekily.

"Not the breed of friends they're looking for, Pat," reared the barkeep, peeved. "You're not—right?" he checked himself.

"No. We seek the *other* sort," Sinon mouthed with blinks.

"Oh! Well, in that case, wouldn't know nothing about that," he clamed up in a tense voice and a blushed face and set to scram.

"Stoop down," she told. He bent. She whispered in his ear.

He listened with a grave face. She slipped few thousand bucks in his hand. The cash seemed to creäte a great effect on the barkeep: his face convulsed; his right eye spasmed; thick brows furrowed; lips pressed; chin raised. "Your money's no good." He scrunched the cash in Sinon's face, threw the wad on the floor, and squished them with polished boot. His lips quivered in white rage. "Leave when you've drank your drinks." He stomped to the bar. Sinon watched him go with a cold eye that gauged the state. She picked the notes, smoothed the angry creases, and shoved them back in her pocket. She sank back in her seat, crinkled her nose, pursed her lips, and arched a brow. Adam gave himself theatrical airs at the sight of it all. The drunk rasped in chuckles; chugged his glass with a *glug-glug* and belched. The old man in mended clothes was on edge; he stood, leant on the bar with dignity, and did his coat. He was small, frail, pale. He cleared his throat and toddled over, drink in hand; bent double as though he beards a weight.

"May I impose on the kind couple? Pat's the name, short for Patrick," the man said in a garbled speech. Adam jumped to feet and pulled a chair. The old man crouched to the seat with effort, with a "Phew!" Then he looked about absentmindedly, as though he had forgotten what he had come over to do or say.

"We are not a couple," Sinon said in a blasé way.

"We are alone—together," Adam, put out, put in.

After gaping at Adam for a time, "Eek!" awed the old man, jolted aback, taken back by Adam's scars. "What's with his face?"

"It's nothing," said he, pulling over the tuque on his head.

The old man edged an eye to Sinon. "What's with his face?"

"War?" she said off-the-cuff, with a wink, tongue in a cheek.

"Ah! Well, war's an ugly thing, to be sure of that; for sure: *very* ugly," held the old man as he shuffled feet so that his small body pivoted in the seat, inch by inch, to face away from Adam.

When the old man's eye, in turn, set on Sinon, her beauty caught his breath as much as Adam's mug had. "Now you! my dear, are a looker," he said and kissed the tips of a hand's fingers outward. "Dirty young man, are you?" she reacted; a tad harsh.

Bemused, the old man was. Wrinkles wrapped his bronzed face. His gray eyes, half covered with eyelids, fanned in wrinkles. His white, grizzled hair, eyebrows, sideburns, and beard grew out like a coarse wool. Clearly, he had not bathed for some time. His skin-and-bones, callused, crusty hands had black dirt packed in their lines and chipped nails.

"No, it's true," said the man. "I'm a scamp," he hit his head. "Men are. For the good that I would, I do not: but the evil which I would not, *that I do*. But I've found most women to be just as— dirty." Sinon, all haughty, crossed her legs.

"No, it's true. Women have better minds for it. They cheat just as much—if not more. See a woman is upright only when not tempted—by chance; vice has no better doer than chance. And it is worse for a man, to boot. People look down on a chump with a two-timing wife with contempt—as a patsy—when he knows it, more than ever. Some, even, send husbands flowers at work!"

"All right, Mr." She waved a hand. "Why don't you go back to where you came from. We're waiting for friends," she added; then downed her moonshine in two quick gulps. Adam sniffed his glass and repulsed by it held it out at an arm's length; but then downed it. It burnt his throat. All at once, that one glass made him drunk; he was seeing snakes. The drink's effects were on Sinon's flushed face as well; her bloodshot eyes twinkled.

"In those regards," said the old man, "you must forgive my friend." He turned a stiff neck to the bar. "See, he lost his son—"

"Patrick!" the barkeep gave out a caution from the bar. The old man grinned in a cunning like a rascal dog found at mischief.

The tan suit had reached the point when drunks grunt and turn physical. Sinon rapped the table and eyed round as if she ran the odds and grasped: they had come to the wrong place. The drunkard winked at her with a sassy sneer.

"That's it! let's go," she said in a sharp tone and got up.

When leaving, the drunk, with a red face and a vacant look, slurred "Honey" and lurched to grab her arm. She pulled back, reared a punch, but Adam seized her by the arm in time; and he dragged her out as she, writhing to tear off, stretched her arms to the drunk, and cursed. Out of the bar she cooled heels by shaking the ick out of her body. The wails of the drunk rose thru the door: "WHERE IS SHE! HONEY! MY HONEY! WHERE'S MY HONEY!" Sinon cried in reflex. She hid her face in her hands and let off a drawn-out laugh. Adam had kept his mouth shut. Now, he released the dam, burst to a chortle, and split his sides. From across the empty road the black shoeshine-boy yelled. "SHINING SHOES. GET YOUR SHOES SHINED. SHOESHINE." Sinon's eyes sparkled, and her head set engrossed on the boy. She pulled her sleeves and said: "Let's go".

As they crossed the asphalt jungle the boy tapped a step with a shoe brush. He did not look up at them but at their shoes with a pearly, toothy smile. The boy donned a grey newsboy cap; an oversized, threadbare brown shirt with its sleeves rolled up; an undersized black pants with big patches on its knees; and worn shoes with holes taped and covered with black shoe polish. He had a round, freckled, sharp face; and with small brown eyes that had a proud, bold look.

"Like your shoes shined, Mistuh—Ma'am? Name's Sarge—short for Sergeant—can call me Sarge. Took the line of work from Mr Patrick." From his back he brought out a large placard of Pat sitting at that corner holding up a shoe and a shoe brush with a broad smile; scrawled on it in black: "Patrick!" Adam and Sinon had to strain to pull their laugh. She composed herself and said: "We would love to have our shoes shined, Sarge," and nudged Adam. He looked at her questioningly. She pointed him with her eyes to the boy's step. Adam peered at his new brown boots, and, surprised to see them scuffed, raised up a boot on the boy's step.

"What's with the twin getup; cute couple, are you?" asked the boy as he set out to polish shoe.

"We're not—"

"—a couple"

"We were fixing to go on a hike," she harried to a claim. She pulled up her hoodie's hood over her head. "It is a nice day," she added. Then looked up and saw all the smoke pour up from the buildings so high her hood fell back.

"Hike in the middle of a war zone?" the boy screwed up an eye. He bowed back to polish. "Some may take Y'all for spooks."

"Spies! ha! Ha!" she cried and turned a jumpy eye at Adam; he raised his brows and shrugged. Sinon squatted to the boy and waited to catch his eye. "We're looking for our friends. Maybe you know them?" she poked him. "My name's Sinon. And this is Adam."

"What the deuce! *Adam*?" the boy jolted at them in a shock. "Is that short for Adamah?"

"Yes; that's right!" Sinon's face glowed at the boy's reaction.

"Aright, aright, aright—that's alright. Belike, Y'all sized me up from yon the road, and thought, Let's put one over ol' Sarge there. Tell Ya what, strait: you were *dead wrong*. I've lived a long life, here and there; and no one can hoodwink ol' Sarge."

"Why do you say that Sarge? He really is Adam."

"So, The One looks like an extra in a set of a zombie movie?

That doesn't jibe." The boy guffawed. "And I'm the son of Zoro-aster!"

Adam winced and flung a hand. "What is this? Who is this? Who the hell do you think you are?"

Sinon pulled a face. She fixed a glare on Adam and signed for him to stop; but he turned his head and imitated to not have noticed. Riled by the boy's insolence he had ignored that he saw he was a no one.

"He was flogged, Sarge," she rushed a cover.

"For real?" Wonder came over the boy's face.

"Should see my back," Adam cut in, all cross.

"With his stripes we are healed," she quoted. "Bear in mind the Scriptures, Sarge. We just escaped. And we don't have much time. Soon, this place is going to be crawling with Red Helmets and Red Dragons looking for Adam." The words "Red Helmets and Red Dragons", which Sinon voiced in gloom, gave the boy a start. Then his face twitched as he turned a prying eye on each of them as he worked it out. "Wait here" he said, took out a walkie-talkie, and ducked round the corner.

Adam read Sinon's face at a glance and a wink.

After the boy had gone for a few minutes, he rushed back. "All right, then. Y'all can stay with us—till we check you out."

They grasped that what the boy spoke was in keeping with commands.

It was an old, dilapidated house of half wood, half brick with thin windows. Sunk on a side, it tottered by a crater in the yard. One could just make it for dense ivy had creeped and strangled it. Its windows had mildewed panes and beige sheets as for drapes. In the inside it was a dreary, dark house filled with stuff of all sorts. It was the shot, damp, stinky, squatters' house of Pat and Sarge.

Sarge guided Adam and Sinon each to a room; with sheets hung for doors since they had had long burned all the doors as for firewood. Pat set chairs in a fleck of clear spot in the living room. He then sat in front of Sinon, and so close that their knees bumped. Sarge, squat by the fireplace, engrossed in a cream-leaved book, tapped foot. Adam had just asked Pat what had gone on in the city.

"Well, it's hard to say," said the old man and began a fireside tall tale. In the fireplace a warm fire blazed and snapped. "In all the places there was life and joy. There was laughter in the air. Bands and buskers played the streets and squares. Friends called out and hugged. Couples, hand in hand, went in and out of cafés, bookstores, and theatres, till the crack of dawn. What a life it was! But there were dark forces at work here and in other places set to rule. The new PM had run on a 'Country First!' and a 'Take Back Country!' crusade; and, with a shred of Russian meddling, had won the vote. He had run on law, order, and freedom—his own ideas of them. His ruse was to make oaths to all, each of whom felt they could play him. Day he took rule, all cheered, feeling he was their man. Others held: Weight of the office of the PM will restrain the man. Besides, what can he do that is so bad? They were prudent to not bare how extreme their schemes were. They carried out their plan, bit by bit, one red pill by one; with a short pause after each to see if it had been too big of a gulp; then, doled out larger and larger, more on more red pills. They barred them rights of gays, abortion rights, free speech, and the free press. And these were shameless liars. They called real news fake and their fake news real. They claimed that they were taking down a deep state, as they built one. So-called Christians laid hands on the PM and cried out he was King and Christ. Many played on that it was all the fault of China; after all, they got a sweet tax cut.

Folks said this won't last; that this, too, shall pass. Then came the House Fire. By the end of his term the PM had firmed up power. He had his pals placed as heads of armed forces and spy services. Folks went to polls in mass and cast him out. The PM cried the vote (which he tried to rig) rigged and refused to step down. The day of the new PM swearing in, armed forces stormed the senate. Brown shirt jackboots turned up in the armband of a red dragon; hung the new PM and all members not for them; and burnt the House. Next day brought closures and martial law. And the day after that, the German armed forces rolled up. The Red Guards kicked a file down the streets with jutted chins. The PM had had sworn an oath to Hitler and had made a pact with him, Stalin, and Mussolini. There was gory house-to-house fight. They wiped out cities that fought back. Maimed bodies lay in pools of blood on the streets and on stretchers draped with bloody white sheets. They raped; and bombed the hospitals to form a sense that there was no safe space. Jews and Blacks were not to work, own stuff, go in a bus, stores, or sit on benches. They searched, made lists, detained. Non-whites forced to slave work and lived in ghettos; or, tortured and killed in prisons and in camps. Rumours of eyes gouged out and hands cut spread. It was a crime to print and sell books by non-whites; they held book burning bashes. Factories shut. There was no bread, no fuel. Folks said they had seen plane loads of gold fly; they'd seized the bank gold reserves. Then the value of currency sank; the prices of things soared. The stores sat bare as looted. A pipe cost more than a whole house that you'd bought. A bar of soap cost ten thousand one day, sixty the next. Starved folks wore sacks and dragged their feet. At first, people stockpiled cash; then, they exchanged like Stone Age cave men. Folks fled homes to the country or went in the under—" There was a loud knock at the front door. All sprung to feet and stuck a pose, with wild eyes. Pat put a finger to nose and turned to the door. Sarge hid his book in the floor. Then came soft taps: *rat—tat*. Pat and Sarge sighed in big relief. "Ah, it's him," said Sarge in a tone which hinted that they knew the knocks. Sarge opened the door. And in stepped the Watchman.

Adam, knocked for six, called out, "It's him!"

In his grey frock, the Watchman stood at the front door and eyed the company. In a dash, he ran to Adam, fell on knees, and kissed Adam's boots. "Forgive my sin, Master" he bawled. "I—I can never forgive myself," he claimed in his low-pitched voice.

"You can speak!" said Adam, thrown.

"Yes, Good Master. The vow of silence is just for my cover." Sinon looked coldly at him.

"Why do you call me good..." Adam started but then he saw Sinon's eyes and dropped it. "What sin?"

"Should've known it was you right when I saw you; but I..., and, and I made a..." he left off and did not say he made *a what*.

"I thought I read that... You're with the Underground?"

The Watchman, at last, raised his head, and gazed at Adam with a childlike face. "Yes, Good Master. Must make haste. Red Helmets scour the city." He rose, ran to the door, and stood keen.

Pat shook Adam's hand with two hands and a bowed head. "You touched my heart, sir. You brought me to tears and touched my heart," he cried while he avoided looking up at Adam's face. "Thanks," Adam said. "And Sarge," he turned to the shoeshine-boy. Sergeant said: "Later, Son."

The Watchman's eyes rested on Sinon with attention. "Only you, Master," he blurted out in an awkward way.

"She's coming; wouldn't be here if it wasn't for her." Sinon looked at the Watchman with an unfriendly eye. The Watchman looked uneasy; but, at the same time, he bent his head, faithfully.

Chapter Five

The Underground

As Adam left the house, he saw two Black Helmets at its door and drew back. And there was a black cube van parked by the house.

"Don't fret, sir. They're with us," the Watchman said. Then, he opened a back door of the van; and, with a hand, signed for Adam and Sinon to hop in the van. For a beat, they peeked in the van and at each other edgy. With crossed fingers she was the first to go in. The Watchman gave them grey frocks and ID cards and shut the door. In a pinch, he opened the door. "Put those on. And get some rest; we have a journey ahead." In the van it was pitch dark; it had a small window, and it was small. Adam took off his hoodie and put on the frock. "Use the hoodie to rest your head," she said. Burned out, soon, they fell fast asleep.

Adam woke up. He peeked out of the rain specked window; saw waterspouts spinning from the sky; and, startled, he shook Sinon with "Look! Look!" She banged the front screen of the van.

"We're here!" said the Watchman, ecstatically.

"Where?" they both yelled.

"Necropolis."

Adam and Sinon looked as though they were going to end the Watchman right then and there. "Why did you bring me back here?" Adam barked, restraining himself with effort.

"We are as good as dead," Sinon muttered.

"Trust me, Good Master," he said, dumbfounded.

"You can shove your good master you know where." Adam had more choice curses, but they were pulling up to the gates of hell.

"Must be quiet, Master," said the Watchman, chagrined.

Adam, stooped, knitted his black brows and glared in fear. Sinon's eyes and nose flared; her lips pressed hard to a line.

The van paused at a guardhouse. Black Helmets cleared the van through. They crept a long, narrow passage, then parked by a door marked in black with STAFF.

The front doors of the van slammed. The Watchman opened the back door and glanced pale and coyly in their faces. "You are new and on your first day of training. Please play along," he said, timidly. "Put on your frocks' hoods and keep your heads down."

"Where are you taking us?" Sinon asked with a drawn brow and crossed arms.

The Watchman replied in an excited undertone: "There are two ways to the underground. One is the long way round by land and sea. The other is through the caves below. We are taking the shortcut."

Adam went through an instant change: from rage to shame. Sinon's eyes narrowed and flipped as if new thoughts dawned on her. She left the van with an icy air. Adam tailed her and side-stepped the Watchman (who led in the front; trailed by the Black Helmets). The staff door opened to a long concrete hall with neon lights and steel doors. Black Helmets and Watchmen lined that hall three or four abreast like a swarm of black and grey termites.

The passing Black Helmets and Watchmen bumped them, right and left. The Watchman read the card reader of a door with NS-32 marked on it with black ink. As soon as the door slid open a stream of warm air struck them. They were now in a cave with a bottomless pit of about a hundred feet wide; with a miners' cage attached down the side of it. They crammed in the rusting cage and the Watchman rolled its door and pressed a button. The cage screeched in its fast glide down. Sinon cringed and put fingers in her ears. An avalanche of stone leapt off, clattered and riffed in loud, sharp echoes. As they dropped, the conduit's rock walls drew close, and it grew dark. Fixed and spaced on the rock walls were orange bulbs in a steel mesh and feet markers. As the cage reached bottom it rocked to a stop. In five minutes, they had gone down three thousand feet. They got out and walked to a passage which slanted to their right. They then snaked low stone shafts that went in turns through a series of archways lit by a chain of red lamps. From time to time, Watchmen passed by on affairs of their own. Bodies drifted in streams that shone by the twinkling red lamps. At a fork Adam saw the fox hole he'd seen with keep out tape and caution posts. The Watchman made signs to the two Black Helmets to keep watch; and to Adam and Sinon to stick to him. And with a couple of backward glances round, he crawled in the hole. Adam and Sinon, on guard and in two minds, clawed in after him: Sinon then Adam. It was a dark and dreadfully long and a quite a tight lava tube with sharp juts. The Watchman lit a red glow stick. In that short time, like a mole, he'd managed to sweep far in the shaft. Adam feared closed spaces; he knew that, now. Sinon wedged an arm that held a glowstick back with, "He left ones for us"; and then lighted hers. Adam followed suit. He noted Sinon's rear which arched and swayed as she wriggled. He mused on how he had carnal sense, still, given—well, you know.

Maybe it's like pulled teeth and amputated limbs which ache, he thought.

"You best not be looking at my butt. Are you looking at my butt?" she voiced and coiled her head to him, as though she read his thoughts.

"*What...?*" he let out in a high voice; only thing he could say. As they crawled forward the pipe became narrower; it was so constricting that their arms sealed to their body. They wiggled, inch by inch, by the squirms of their heads, shoulders, and fingers. He began to sweat fiery lava may heave up the snug tube, as well. His heart raced. Panic set in. And then he broke down to an all-out panic attack. "Can't take this! Can't take it! I can't breathe," he cried, gravely alarmed, with a ceased chest, lungs, and heart.

Sinon stopped and told him, "Wait!" She then yelled, "How much farther," to the Watchman far ahead.

"Chut!" the Watchman shushed back. "We're almost there."

She tried to soothe Adam, with her soft, sugary voice. "Hear that, Adam? Pull it together. Just a bit further. You can do this."

"Okay, *okay*," he said, wan looking. He rocked and smacked his head on the rock wall. Then, begged, "*Please* let's go faster."

They then pulled and squeezed up the tube at a hastened pace. And, in the front, the Watchman had got a big stone from the wall and pushed it ahead. In the heart of that cramped pipe the Watchman had revealed a hole which led out of it; but to where? To a further tunnel as they found out when they reached the Watchman and dropped to it. He then pulled the stone back in place by handles attached to it. "We've supplies in here," said the Watchman. He switched on a floodlight that brought to light the roomy tunnel (bit more like a cave with a domed top). Adam sighed. The Watchman set a camp stove. Stored there were water tanks, food, and sacks. They drank water and filled water bottles.

The Watchman made soup from two cans; they ate it in a hurry. The Watchman gave them backpacks with each one stocked with a sleeping bag; rope; a pickaxe; food cans; two crank flashlights; a compass; and a first aid kit. He carried his own pack. And they set off on a slow and windy descent into that chasm. At the start, the slope of the shaft was just apparent; but then it got more and more steep. In the front, the Watchman went on as if he were on the flat. Adam and Sinon slipped over loose stone, scrambled on rock, and stumbled a way through. They cranked the flashlights, often; with the deep dark a few feet before them, at all times. As they went, the duct's thick, bubbled lava glittered with the lights. The burrows knew no end and were too complex to recall. There were runs of sharp turns and archways to other ways. Now and then right by their feet there were large crevices or dark pits; that was the one danger: they may not see a crevasse till they came to it and put a foot in a void. The Watchman did not use a compass for which way to go; and kept a close eye on them; and, at times, would lend a hand. Sinon, on the other hand, eyed her compass on the go; and, at each turn piled stones as for markers. Once the Watchman pointed to a pile, she said, "In case we lose you," and he shook his head and went. (He seemed to have lapsed back to being a mute.) They marched on with no other word. Their steps kicked up dust and stones. A shower of stones bounced the walls to the depths with dull echoes. The lava on the walls gave way to pink and ash marbles with white and black veins and spots. By this time, they had had gone on and on along the unending cave. They came to an open space; first, the Watchman, who switched on a floodlight; then, Sinon and Adam, on their hands and knees. They drank from water jugs kept there and refilled their bottles. The Watchman made soup, again; and they all gobbled it down. The Watchman eyed at Adam with an injured yet a puffed pride.

Adam found that Sinon eyed him, too; and all high and mighty. Adam felt a pang of conscience. He polished his bowl, stood, and went and sat by the Watchman; and bent close to him to signal a heart-to-heart. "I'm so sorry for my words, in the van. I was—crass—no doubt—rude." While Adam came over to sit with him and spoke to him, the Watchman kept his head down. But then he raised his head and glanced up at Adam. His hard face grew kind. He began to say, "I quite understand that..." Ceased with a catch in his throat. And then said, "S—sir," with a red face. A look of great warmth swapped the Watchman's wounded face. There was a long silence, which was awkward for everyone. With an unease of a wake, Adam rose and sat beside Sinon. He looked at her as if asking if he had done it right. Sinon nodded her head with such sweetness it seemed mawkish. The Watchman said it was time to go to sleep; and they got out the sleeping bags with a cheer and fell to sleep without a snore. But before Adam fell to a sound sleep, he thought he heard a muffled sound like that of a leak trickling in a wall. They woke and took up the plunge. As before, the deep dark stretched out, nonstop, just to their front. And Sinon made her stone pyramids at each fork. Adam stopped for her, every time; but the Watchman would keep going and Adam terrified of losing the Watchman would urge her. "Leave me off," she would snap with a hand, each time. They were going thru a granite gallery with twists and turns of a maze. And tens of thousands of feet of stone was above their heads. And as they went a lot of something else ran above their heads: in the walls and around the dark. Water roared about them. The stone floor fell to a vast cleft gaped to unknown depths. The Watchman told Sinon and Adam to stay with an admonitory gesture of a hand.

At their feet waters ripped, leapt, and, with a thundering, rumbling swoosh, vanished. Adam leaned over the edge of the fall to gaze down. The light of his torch pierced a few feet of the fall; beyond which was blind void. (There is *nothing* dodgier than this dumb need to see down deep, dark holes.)

"Be careful," Sinon warned and quaked all over.

Just then, his foot skid on a slick rock, and he fell forwards. Sinon grasped the back of his backpack with a swift hand and broke his fall. She held him up at an acute angle on the edge of the precipice. A shoulder strap crept off; she gripped his pack with both hands; he teetered, reached to her, the other strap gave way—he fell. Adam sank with bugeyes and backstrokes and with a long-drawn "AA..." that died out in the thick dark dense weir.

"ADAM!" she cried.

The cave bounced her cry back round. *Adam..., Adam..., Adam....* The Watchman had frozen, popeyed. (It all took place in less than no time—and, in parts—else he would have had reacted, surely.)

Adam felt the sickening swift descent, and he saw two zig-zagging beams fade out to black. Air whizzed by in a whistle. "A long way," he thought. Before he knew it, he dunked into rapids. Whiplashed, he heard muffled spray and bubbles rupture. Then, bobbed eddying torrents with a many a spin, bump, thud, and smack, and jostled stones. As Adam binned down the gorge with force he knocked and scraped serrated rock walls. And it all went blank.

~

He felt a smooth pillow and crisp white sheets. He heard a gentle drone of waves that broke on a shore. He breathed in a refreshing breeze coming in from an open window. He opened his eyes. He was in a room of a lodge with white walls and a sailing décor. He looked out of a sliding glass door to a still deep blue sea. He rose in ironed white shirt and pants. He stepped out on hot, fine sand which gave and shifted under foot. At first, with eyes not used to bright light, he squinted; then, he stood with eyes wide open. The sea went to a hazy line in the horizon. A ship in full bubbled sail left a harbour. Waves lapped up a pebbled shore. Lofty cliffs rose to the rear of a city of white homes with coloured windows and doors in front of a line of tall trees. Before it all, vertical granite soared to a vault that spanned a sky (so to speak) puffed in cloud. Falls dove down from those spiky rock walls to babbling streams. Bright light suffused things on all their sides like the rays of sun at noon; but it was not the light of a sun, because it had no heat. Nor was it the dim light of a moon. It was vivid like that of some chemicalization, or that of a dream.

He thought he was in a dream, once more. He slapped himself with a "Wake—up! Wake—up!" Then he saw a woman in a flapping white dress on the beach. She shielded her eyes with a hand and looked out to the sea. She turned, saw him, then said something. He cupped a hand to an ear.

"I said, you're awake," she said as she went to him. She had long black hair, olive skin, high cheekbones, thin eyebrows, big brown eyes, and a soft voice.

"So, this isn't a dream?"

"It sure seems like it, doesn't it," she turned to look back at the glistening sea. She eyed him over a shoulder. "I'm Mary."

"I'm—"

"I know. They found you washed up," she pointed, "there."

"What about Sinon and the Watchman? Where are they?"

She shrugged her shoulders and turned her head each way.

Foam-lined waves spread up the fine sand with a *shh*, then, drew back: *Shh… Shh… Shh… Shh… Shh… Shh… Shh… Shh… Shh….*

A House Not Made with Hands

ADAM LAY in an operating theatre. A kaleidoscope of equipment flashed and beeped. Cables ran every which way. He was on a surgical bed with bright headlights over him. A robotic arm with a microscope tilted itself up and down and side to side. A half-dozen nurses in shields, caps, masks, gloves, and gowns prepped him. By him sat a tray of saws, forceps, scalpels, hooks, spatulas, drills, pans, and an anesthesia machine with displays and tubes. Adam eyed about like a terrified lab monkey.

"Ready for your awakening, Mr Adamah?"

He made the masked voice as Mary's. "You're a doctor?"

"Metaphysician. We're going to administer general anaesthetics now."

She put a gasmask on his face; then, placed a clamp of screw pins on his head and tightened its screws.

"Once you wake up, you *will* remember, *in full*, your past life on Earth."

Adam came to. He was back at the seaside lodge in the same bed and white shirt and pants as before. He sat up. He saw his head in the mirror of a facing dresser wrapped up in so much gauze it looked like he wore a white turban. "Do you remember?" Mary, inquisitively, raising in an armchair by the bed, asked.

It rushed back to him: A grey cat purrs. A fist knocks on a weathered door. A woman in a red summer dress stands on a hill. A small pond in an island shaped like a saddle. An iceberg drifts in a blood-streaked bay. A harpooned whale drags a boat by a stout line. A note signed by Melville: "*This is the book's secret motto—ego non baptiso te in nominee—but make out the rest yourself.*" A cabin with a red "Bung-Your-Eye" sign. Captain Kidd in a cave with a treasure chest. A headless horseman with a drawn sword. A severed head rolls. A rowboat in a thick fog. A Foghorn sounds off. A King James Bible. A glass of water. A glass of wine. A metal capsule falls in a shaft with a *ping*. Men in black suits. A metal needle in his hand. A black helicopter firing its guns. "I do..."

Mary left him at the lodge bar till she came to take him to see the city. The barkeep, with a black tie tucked in a grey dress shirt, kept busy with lemon and glass. A tall man in checked sport coat, blue shirt and tie sat with him at the bar. The man had large ears, blue eyes, slicked back fine hair and spade beard and moustache and ruddy cheeks. He lit a cigarette and ordered a cup of coffee and a bottle of applejack. Adam had had ordered a cup of coffee too. The man whistled while he regarded the barkeep and Adam.

"Bit of frost in your coffee?" he said in a deep voice and held a thin bottle up to Adam. "To give it confidence..."

"No—no thank you. Don't drink. Just remembered that."

"Ah!" he reacted, then poured himself a long spurt of applejack. The man did not query for Adam's name nor Adam for his.

Since he had been born there one thing had bothered Adam. "How is it possible for there to be an ocean up in the sky?"

"Nothing could be easier," said the man; and asked the barkeep for a pint of beer and a clean coaster. He placed the coaster on top of the glass, held it in place, and flipped the glass; then, took his hand off the coaster. To Adam's shock the paper held the whole pint of beer up in the glass. "Simple physics," he held "friction," he added and turned the glass over. Then Adam asked for a tall glass of water and a clean coaster and turned them over. "You've a party trick," said the man, and poured more applejack.

"But what's the coaster up" Adam pointed "there?"

"Glass. In the formative years of this planet magma came to its ocean, which covers the whole of this planet—to sand—at its northern hemisphere; drew back and left a glass basin and—you must be new?" Adam nodded. The man pulled a face and said, "Old spinal injury," held his back, and shot Adam an eye.

"Like to shoot?" he asked Adam, apropos of nothing.

"Guns?"

"Yes; what else."

"Don't know—don't think so."

"Have you considered joining the resistance? We need able-bodied men to fight the fascist commies."

"O, I don't know." (He turned a cold eye on Adam's tuque.)

"You are not one of those hippie types, are you?"

"I think I'm one of those 'they that take the sword perish with the sword' types."

The man mumbled and mumbled: "Dirty, shuffling, drag-ass hippies. Dirty, shuffling hippies, swinging the lead."

Mary came back, saw the man, and said, "Hi Mr Steinbeck."

"John Steinbeck?" Adam snapped, flabbergasted.

"How are your travels?" she asked gaily.

"It's a dog-leg—I mean, it's remarkable. Wonderful!"

"Boy! I wish I could go," she said with a look of longing. Mary and Adam left the lodge. "He looks so young!" Adam said, turning back. "He's been here for thirty years or so," Mary said. Two men left the lodge after them in black suits and at a distance.

Mary led Adam through cobbled streets lined with whitewashed homes and flats that had dyed windows and doors, iron terraces, and steel roofs. The streets, with their gas lamps, led one to new sights and sounds at round each corner. Bookshops, art galleries, little knickknack stores, cafés, and patios. On one turn they went by a small discothèque. Its pink neon sign buzzed "Eden Disco". Adam stopped and said, "I recognize that!" Then went back and peeked in the flashing club. Sylvester was on its stage. He sang "You Make Me Feel (Mighty Real)" in falsetto, and in a red kimono, with a curly hair. He flapped a fan and pointed. Behind him backup dancers in red tank tops and white short shorts grinded and gyrated. Mary pulled Adam by that corner to "Eden Pzazz". On its stage a young Joséphine Baker, in a chic black gown, sang "La Conga Blicoti" and danced. She lay on hips which scooped up with a slinky toe to heel step, wrists on hips. They went on and entered a late-night bohemian café. Jim Morrison's "Awake" played there. She went to a table where a man in his thirties, in a black suit and tie, sat. He was very tall and skinny—wraithlike— broad shouldered; with swept-up wavy black hair; thick, round, black-rimmed glasses on a prominent nose; and one cloudy eye.

Mary circled around Adam and said, "This is Mr Adamah."

"Huxley," said the man, and crossed a long leg on the other.

"Huxley! Aldous Huxley?" cried Adam, stupefied.

"Liked my books?" he asked in a modulated, graceful voice.

"Don't know if that's the right word... One was prophetic."

Huxley dropped his head. "They say you are the prophet." He eyed up and said, "Say hello to my friend," pointing him out. Adam turned, and yet another tall man in his thirties and round, black-rimmed glasses stood before him in a grey suit and purple bowtie. He had a broad forehead; swept-up wavy brown hair; an aquiline nose; and blue eyes with an intense gaze.

"Erwin Schrödinger," said he like an English professor with an aura of culture; sat by Huxley and crossed a leg up on another.

"Erwin Schrödinger!" Adam repeated, dazed.

Mary and Adam sat in front of the two men who looked like brothers if not an express image of one another. She sat straight-backed, with her head inclined to one side. After a moment of silence, as often happens with people who meet for the first time, Huxley said "He doesn't like my books" to Schrödinger in a mannerly nonchalance. Then brushed his sleeves most pedantically.

"Well—it's just that—the characters in some of your novels speak in speeches; and your book on enlightenment is a string of capitalized words and Zen Buddhist nonsense, like, a thing is a thing and not a thing." (Adam noticed Mary cringe and he pulled on his tuque at both ears.) Huxley listened in a patient manner; then, dropped his head and replied with: "Beauty is truth, truth, beauty. Zen majors in nonsense, to bewilder a mind to go beyond sense." He gazed with a look in which there was an awareness of his own superiority. And he brushed off a pleat of his black suit.

There was a burst of laughter at the front door and in came Sylvester and Joséphine Baker. He had on a gold sequin turban and shawl, and she wore a little sheer dress and gelled wavy hair.

"Ooh, we had service!" Sylvester said and sat beside Adam.

Joséphine sat on Huxley's knees, laid back on Schrödinger's lap, and her perky breasts fell out the sides of her dress.

"Who is this!" Sylvester asked Mary and leaned on Adam.

"The one people have been talking about..."

"And what does you say about gays?" he asked, haughtily.

"People who quote St. Paul, on women with women, men with men, skim his main point; in that, *no one* should have sex. Nor marry, because then you will spend all your time on pleasing a spouse and in the care for a family rather than in the pursuit of spiritual understanding. But to prevent—say, reduce fornication, marriage is a stopgap. In any case, the first page of Genesis says God made man male *and* female. (Jesus called it: twain in one)."

Huxley and Schrödinger groped Joséphine; lustily murmuring something-somethings. She lay frozen over them with closed eyes. The two men bore the sleazy smiles of indecent thoughts.

"No sex? Seen that work out for priests," Sylvester scuffed.

"It's not about holding back, and, as St. Paul called it, *burn*; but spiritual understanding that ends the desire and need for it."

"I want—thou shalt," Schrödinger piped up. "It is primitive desire. It is absurd and unnatural to require humans to deny and suppress their primitive urges—to be other than what they are. God is nature. Nature made me as she sees fit—as I ought to be."

"Assuming God has creäted what we call nature. St. Paul pointed out that we've changed man and the animals to our own corrupt imaginations of a god and to carnivorous beasts."

Joséphine rolled her eyes and said, "I'm naturel". Adjusted her dress, rose, and beckoned the two men to leave the bar with her. "This is splendid!—the reason Mary brought you to us. But forgive us, we have a prior engagement," Schrödinger said, with a significant look at Huxley; who showed by a nod of his head that a secret understanding had passed between them, and said: "Perhaps we can do breakfast tomorrow?" Schrödinger replied: "Let's do brunch." Then the three made their adieus, arm in arm.

Adam mused, "What engagement?"

"Ménage à trois," Sylvester said, and got up and left as well.

Adam shook his head. Mary, discretely, evaded his glance.

As Sylvester left, in came Sinon and the Watchman, all worn and begrimed. Adam jumped off his seat as if caught in a wrong-doing. They spied Adam, rushed to him, and hugged in. "Master! Master!" the Watchman skipped with joy. Adam glowed at the thrilled man with welled up, shining eyes.

"We thought you'd died," Sinon said in astonishment.

Adam, shamefaced, with a flushed face that reflected it, had all but forgotten Sinon and the Watchman for a time.

They spoke animatedly, and, in a hurry, to learn what had had gone down since they were split up; and they all had an eye-opener. "We scoured the gorge for two days and gave you up for dead. When they told us you were here, we couldn't believe it," Sinon said.

Mary came to say hi to the Watchman, which she knew, met Sinon, and said: "You must be dying for baths and a good night's rest. We've rooms at the lodge." And with those words, they left.

~

"So, we're in dark matter now?" Adam asked Schrödinger.

"Yes; that is the held theory." Huxley, Sinon, Schrödinger, Adam and Mary sat for brunch in the dining room of the lodge. A self-playing piano played Satie's *Gymnopédie* in a loop. By the sea, a boy threw a log into the water that rippled in wavelets; and after the log disappeared for a beat, it popped out, oscillated, and floated away. Forks, knives, and glasses clanked against plates. Adam noticed the queer fellows in black suits which he had seen earlier sitting at a corner and glancing about surreptitiously with shifty eyes. They listened to the chatter like they did not want to show it. Framed mirrors which hung on all sides copied out their reflections.

"This planet," Schrödinger went on, "is located in the same exact position as Earth with the same planets orbiting a sun in a Milky Way galaxy. On Earth we could account for about five percent of the matter in the universe, only. But here about five percent more has been weighed by—"

"Can we go back to where we had left off?" Huxley butt in. "On whether man creäted God or God man?"

"I would like to know how there can be a King James Bible in my room, first." Adam said and placed the Bible on the table.

"King James, as well as the disciples who'd wrote the Bible on Earth—all of whom had come to violent death—bar St. John— rewrote the Bible here," Mary said. "And the people with photographic memory have confirmed it is word for word; except for the four references in the book of Revelation to John to the second death, which—"

The waiter cut her short to take the table's luncheon orders.

Schrödinger surveyed Adam's menu squints and said, "Do not fret Mr Adamah. No breast milk nor flesh is dished up here."

"All plant-based," Mary said, with an explanatory gesture.

"Oh! Good," Adam reacted, exchanging glances with them.

"Mercy and kindness towards all living beings (not only our fellow-men)—the highest attainable goal: reverence for all life, is easier to attain in this world since there are no animals up here," Schrödinger said.

"No animals?"

"None."

"But I saw a black cat," Adam turned to Sinon (who'd been shifting her bright blue eyes from a speaker to another in a stuck-up, quizzical air, with a shade of disdain). She gave a deep sigh.

Mary started back. "You saw a cat?"

"Yes; a cat."

"You did not see a cat."

"What if I *did* see a cat?"

"You saw the Shapeshifter!" She saw the waiter coming up with a basket of bread; her voice sank to a whisper, and she said: "But let's not speak of her here. I will tell you about her..., later."

"And what does God say about killing and eating animals?" Schrödinger wondered. And all gazed at Adam with curiosity.

"In Genesis, on its first page says...," Adam opened the Bible to its first page. "I have given you every herb bearing seed, which is upon the face of all the earth, and every tree, in the which is the fruit of a tree yielding seed; to you it shall be for meat."

"Brings to mind a poster I saw on Earth of a hunter in camouflage," Schrödinger said, turning his plate and shuffling his fork and knife, "praying over a deer, captioned with the Bible quote: 'Every moving thing that liveth shall be meat for you'."

"'Even as the green herb have I given you all things,' it goes on; then adds: 'But flesh with the life thereof, which is the blood thereof, shall ye not eat'. They'd left out the very next sentences."

With brunch disposed of and coffee served, Mr Huxley pressed Adam, once again. Adam turned to him with a thoughtful penetration and spoke in a low voice as if in the telling of great secrets.

"Ministers don't tell people that there are two distinct parts to Genesis, to the story of creation. Bible scholars call the first part Elohistic, since its God is Elohim; and they call the second part Jehovistic, since its god is Jehovah (Lord God). That the first part which covers the Bible's first page, only, it's Elohim, the real God who creätes; that from the second page on, from where it restarts with: there rose a mist, the second account of creation's given by the man-made god called Jehovah (or Yawah): a tribal king who people must worship with rituals, ceremonies, and special gifts; demands a regular sacrifice of animals and humans; is vengeful, wrathful; provides detailed instructions on how to stone women; and conducts mass murder of animals and humans via plagues, floods, earthquakes, other so-called natural disasters, wars, etc."

An odd look passed between their eyes as though there was no telling what they'll hear from Adam next—other than Sinon, who had a vacant look, as if she dreamt over something else.

"And, what's more, the second chapter is written such that we would know that it is not the real God's creation. God creätes man with His Word in the first chapter; but in the second chapter the Lord God (Jehovah) forms man out of the dust of the ground. Dust here is in its sense of nothingness; as in, dust to dust. Then, the Lord God (Jehovah) induces a deep sleep in Adam to perform a surgical operation on him to take one of his ribs to creäte Eve. It should have been clear that a real God would not have had a need for a rib to make a woman. What's even more outrageous is that most people have taken for real the passage on God having condemned mankind because Adam and Eve ate an apple! The point is that we shouldn't eat the fruit from the tree of good *and* evil; *and* being the operative word since a tree that God creätes is good, and is good, only. 'Either make the tree good, and his fruit good; or else make the tree corrupt, and his fruit corrupt'."

Sinon was now eyeing the men in black suits, boldly, with an assumed ease. But she turned to Adam and, at once, seemed disturbed. "What about Satan?" Interested in the discussion, all of a sudden, she pulled her sleeves up, menacingly. "Does Satan exist?" (She pronounced Satan with a special emphasis on the *s*.)

"God, to be God, must have foreknowledge: knowledge of the future; otherwise, like us, he'd be prone to accidents. Having foreknowledge, He would have known that by creäting an angel named Lucifer, He would have, then, had creäted Satan, as well. But, then again, He may not have foreknowledge, and the Devil would have had crafted evil *in and of himself*; with Satan conjuring up a coequal—if not a more superior—power to Gôd. But 'if a kingdom is divided against itself that kingdom cannot stand'."

"Does he exist or not?" She looked Adam up like a stranger.

"Not if there is *one* God, the *good*. Since, for Satan to exist God would have had to intend for another, opposing power, and God would have had to impart the knowledge of evil to Lucifer. God is light, and in him there is no darkness at all."

"What about the notion that God is testing us?"

"Again, with God having foreknowledge the test would be worthless since He would know the answer to the test before the act of creation; He would know all your decisions, beforehand."

"But the test is for us to learn and grow."

"But, since the beginning of mankind up to now, how many people would you say have gained spiritual understanding and reached the understating that Jesus had? A handful..., perhaps?"

"If that," Mary said, inclining her head to one then the other.

"Then, we can all agree that a test, if there were such a test, is useless." Adam pounded a fist on the table like a judge's gavel. "And what are animals supposed to learn from all their misery?" (Adam was like a man long kept in a quarantine, who was now set free to assert himself; and he spoke with such an authority no one could tell if what he was saying was first-rate or second-rate.)

"Who says the goal is to be Christlike?" asked Huxley, with his level-headed, gray-eyed, mirror-like gaze.

"Because that's true Christianity. Churches have cheapened Christianity to sayings, like: I accept Jesus Christ as my Lord and Saviour; as if it's a magic incantation. Or Jesus died for *our* sins;

never mind the fact that, as Paul pointed out, the entire point of Christianity is that: Jesus *didn't* die."

There was a disappointed silence. Sinon, sunk into her chair with arms slung over the chair handles, had her eyes glazed over.

"Is knowing what Jesus knew realistic?" Huxley sneered; as if, at last, he had made up his mind to prove Adam's foolishness.

"If not, then, his teachings and works were in vain. But he said: 'They that believe in me, the works that I do they shall do also; and greater works than these shall they do'."

Sinon pinched the bridge of her nose; said she had a headache and had to rest. She rose and, for a moment, eyed herself in a mirror in a twisted pose with puckered lips. (Adam saw a flash of mischief in her look.) She yanked her sleeves up still higher; ran fingers in her hair; sent an airborne kiss into the mirror; and, with an *"Au revoir"* twirled quickly and quickly left. The mirrors on the walls echoed the men in black, who eyed the mirror where Sinon had just been, twisting and bending to look at her leaving.

"Is not this salvation by knowledge worse than salvation by grace which springs up not from one's own merits? Salvation by knowledge is worst because it not only requires intelligence but also leisure, for meditation; and the advantage goes not only to the intelligent but to those wealthy with all the time to devote to metaphysical speculation," Schrödinger contemplated.

"We would have a lot of time if we weren't forever busying ourselves, because we cannot sit in a room, quietly, with our own thoughts. At all times, our minds stray with idiotic, negative self-talk. So, we strive to find some pursuit to save us from our own thoughts: some with careers, money, and power; some with sex and affairs; some with sports; some with their cars; some with the killing of animals as a sport; some with animal-abusing rodeos, zoos and aquariums; yet some with parties, drinking, and drugs.

Or they do what they do because of boredom; people bore easily. But the point is that: all desire and like sinning, openly or on the sly; deceiving, and being deceived. And all make excuses for evil; as in, if there were no evil would we know what good is? Every domain of human life, even its so-called good, is bound up with duplicity and evil. In any case, most wouldn't want a reality with only good choices." (The men in black left the diner. They were the only ones left in the diner. A waiter refilled cups with coffee. The pianola keyed out Satie's atmospheric melodies, still.)

"What about the intelligence that is needed?"

"Humans are, basically, Neanderthals—with smart thermo-stats. But earlier, I believe you were saying we've accounted for only ten percent of all matter in the universe?"

"Astrophysicists have calculated the weight of the universe to be composed of roughly seventy percent energy; the rest being matter. If matter's divvied in five percent, there are six worlds," Schrödinger said, guessing where Adam was heading. The long-burning fire in Adam's eyes grew brighter and brighter.

"So, if one doesn't gain spiritual understanding on Earth—most will not—then, they will, eventually, gain it in some future-world. People think the book of Revelation's about some world-wide event that'll occur for all, simultaneously. But Jesus said the kingdom of God will not be coming with observation because the kingdom of God is within us."

"But what is it we are to understand?" Huxley annunciated, with his glassy, hypnotic gaze.

Adam leaned in. "What I'm about to tell kings and princes have desired to know since the beginning." He perused the table with flashing eyes. "The material world is a projection of human consciousness, which constructs–deconstruct our bodies and the world *out there*. Being human is like a sleeping dream, an Adam-dream, where we wander in a maze of consciousness. The comatose state goes on with our eyes closed or open. When asleep and dreaming, the material world of our dreams is as real to us as the smoothness of these plates, the hardness of this table, the feel of coarse sand beneath our—"

"This is foolish wordplay!" Schrödinger cried with gusto. "Are you dreaming me and everything else, and am I dreaming you and everything else, so cleverly that our dreams match?"

"Yes! the collective human consciousness's making it all up. As one of the most well-known fathers of quantum physics, you discovered that until observed, atoms, the building blocks of all matter, do not manifest themselves as physical objects; that until observed atoms are statistical probability waves. Physicists can't have a double-minded view of the world: on the one hand taut quantum mechanics as scientific fact, but on the other insist on atoms that are never observed."

"Are you saying Jesus said this?" Mary asked.

"Jesus was the original quantum physicist. He didn't turn water into wine to condone drinking alcohol. He didn't walk on water, make storms disappear and fish appear out of thin air, to show off as a prophet. He was demonstrating consciousness projects everything." (Adam placed a special emphasis on the *everything*.) "Brains don't creäte consciousness; consciousness creätes matter, brains, bodies, etc." Huxley raised a hand, seemed like he was in the throes of a sniping comment, was about to say something, but dropped his head, as though struck dumb, and pressed his lips. Schrödinger looked about in wonder and in incredulity.

Mary cast an eye round as though the tables might have ears and whispered: "But did Jesus and his disciples say any of this?"

"Every time before Jesus raised someone from the dead, he said they were not dead, but that they were just *sleeping*. And all through the New Testament we read: 'Awake thou that sleepest and arise from the dead'. 'Now's high time to awake out of sleep'. 'But now is Christ risen from the dead and become the firstfruits of them that slept'. And Jesus kept saying 'I am not of this world'. 'My kingdom is not of this world'. And said, 'That which is born of the flesh is flesh; and that which is born of the Spirit is spirit'. All over the New Testament it says: 'They which are the children of the flesh, these are not the children of God'. 'Are ye so foolish? having begun in the Spirit, are ye now made perfect by the flesh?' 'But ye are not in the flesh, but in the Spirit.' 'Born, not of blood, nor of the will of the flesh, nor of the will of man, but of God.' Jesus said, 'God is Spirit.' Not a sprite or a ghost, but pure consciousness. He said, 'Except a man be born again, he cannot see the kingdom of God. Except a man be born of water and of the Spirit, he cannot enter into the kingdom of God. Marvel not that I said unto thee, Ye must be born again.' Water signifies purity; so, we must cleanse ourselves, turn good, and purify our hearts. Re-read the New Testament and you will see it in a new light. In his first epistle to Corinthians, Paul says: 'As we have borne the image of the earthy, we shall also bear the image of the heavenly. Now this I say, brethren, that flesh and blood cannot inherit the kingdom of God; neither doth corruption inherit incorruption. Behold, I shew you a mystery; we shall not all sleep, but we shall all be changed'. 'In a moment, in the twinkling of an eye, at the last trump: for a trumpet shall sound, and the dead shall be raised incorruptible, and we shall be changed'. 'Being born again, not of corruptible seed, but of incorruptible, by the word of God'. A trumpet will sound (like the ringing of an alarm clock), and we will awake; this illusion of our consciousnesses vanishes, and we will find ourselves in God's consciousness: in reality. 'For ye are dead, and your life is hid with Christ in God'."

Huxley, as though divining a thought, asked, "What about evolution?" He peered challengingly into Adam's eyes. "Do you believe in the evolutionary theory?" He winked at Schrödinger.

Adam, with a free-and-easy air, replied: "I do."

"How can it be!" Schrödinger cried, confounded, crossing one leg high over the other, seemingly unable to believe his ears. "Is not Darwin's theory of evolution and Christianity contradictory?"

"Not at all. As long as one is in a dream and never questions the reality of that dream, the rules and laws of the dream apply and seem *very* real—until one awakens, or, unless one has a lucid dream."

The company sighed, shook head, crossed and, or recrossed their legs, and marvelled at Adam.

~

It was night—well, at least Adam figured it was night since there was no sun to set in that clockless, sunless netherworld; its eerie luminescence was like that of Earth's Arctic Circle midnight sun.

Earlier, he had gone to check on Sinon. He had knocked on her door and called out her name, quietly, at first; but, when there was no answer, he'd redoubled his knocks with a hard, loud *tat-tat* of a knock; but yet, he'd received no answer. So, figuring that she was beat from the journey and asleep, still, he had left her be.

He was on the beach, barefooted. An expanse of a blue sea stretched out before him; its shore widened as far as eyes could discern. Waves broke incessantly. He lay beneath a vast vault of stupendous rock excavation. The soaring, over-arched leagues of tremendous rock weighed on him, terribly. He felt all bound up, as if that ever-receding vault were now moving ever lower to an oppressive crypt. He sat up, with arms around raised knees. He was mulling the adage of not casting one's pearls on those who would trample them when he saw men in black suits approaching from his left and right, hemming him in. He roused himself, got up, and threw his head side to side with frightened, questioning eyes. The men cried, madly, from each direction, with drawn guns.

"GET ON THE GROUND—"

"—GET ON THE GROUND—"

"—ON THE GROUND—NOW!"

The smallest and least fierce of the men stepped in front of Adam with narrowed eyes. Adam put his hands up and looked around, wildly, in a fright, as though he could scarcely understand what they demanded of him. Suddenly arms seized him from the back in a tight-fisted chokehold; before he knew what was happening, he slammed onto the sand. And from that moment on everything whirled about. They fell on him with threats, shouts, and swears, and heaved their full weight upon Adam's back with their knees and hands. He came to his senses and took in the position he was in.

"STOP RESISTING YOU PIECE OF SHIT!"

"GIVE ME YOUR HANDS!"

"STOP RESISTING!"

They were bending and twisting Adam's arms behind his back. He wanted to say he was not resisting but could not bring it out. He could not get air. His face worked in convulsively and turned apoplectic red. They almost broke his arms and wrists, but they managed to cuff his hands behind his back and rolled him over to his side. Several of the men forcibly dragged Adam under the arms to an awaiting car, which sped off through narrow, cobbled streets.

Adam, ensconced between two sturdy-looking men in the car's back seat, scared stiff, searched all over with his eyes. The city was all in astir, as though for a battle. Well-groomed soldiers which held rifles with fixed bayonets kicked in the streets, everywhere, like actors with jut out chins.

The car turned to a gritty access road at the back of a nondescript brick building. The building's interior matched its exterior.

The men took Adam inside, then to a tiny room with a two-way mirror on one wall and an orange table and two chairs and locked him in. The rectangular orange table had a big metal bar affixed to it on one end.

Adam had made up his mind to give a piece of his mind to whomever had ordered his uncalled-for arrest. And he paced up and down the room, rapidly, glaring, now and then stopping and sternly pointing off a wall with cuffed hands.

A man in black opened the door, catching Adam unawares. Not knowing what he was to say or do, Adam tore off his tuque, and threw it on the floor. After a pause, Adam, with flaring eyes, not knowing why he had done that, stamped a foot on the tuque. Adam's baffling performance stopped up the man in his tracks. But after he stood and looked directly at Adam with fixed, wide-open eyes (Adam felt the man read him through and through) he came in the interrogation room, eyeing Adam, with disdain. He gave Adam a false smile—with his mouth, not with his eyes. He sat on a chair; then frowned at Adam, as if asking: "Why are you standing?" Adam picked up his tuque, then sat, facing the two-way mirror. The man was dark-skinned, grim-looking; with high cheekbones and wide-set, narrow, menacing eyes. He set two big files on the table: one had Adam's name on it, the other Sinon's.

"Mr Adam. How long have you known this Sinon woman?" asked the man in a measured, dry voice, articulating each word.

"Not long." A great gloom fell on Adam, as though anticipating being on the brink of some ruin.

"How long, for instance?" he asked, testily, nostrils flaring.

"A few days."

"So, you've been working together for only a few days?"

"Don't know if that's what you call it. She's a friend."

"What do you and your friends call your cell?"

"*Cell?*"

"Your group—team: fellow conspirators," he said in intense hatred.

"What group? What team?"

"You can drop the act, now, Mr Adam." He heaved back in his chair in condescension.

"It's Adamah."

"You can drop the act, now, Mr—whatever you call yourself. My men spotted your partner entering the caves. I want you to know that we *will* catch up to her before she reaches the subsurface." (Adam's spirit sank at each word.) "She gave her detail the slip, and has about a three-hour head start, but they will..." he did not say *will what* but suffice it to say he meant to catch her.

"Did you make waymarkers in those tunnels, on the way?"

Adam grew grave; what dawned on him, now, shook him.

"Sinon waymarked the way. They were in case we got lost."

"No honour among tittle-tattling traitors, eh, Mr *dim—ha*?"

The man was belligerent. Either he was hostile because he had to interrogate Adam, or he was down on Adam because he was hostile by nature; none the less, the man was hostile. And it was clear he liked being pissy and desired to dig up more ground so he can be even more pissy.

"It's *Adamah*. I'm *not* a traitor. Where's the Watchman?" The Watchman was the only one that could have told them about the markers. The man screwed up an eye, slyly. "We started with *his* interrogation, first. He seems to think you are his master..."

"Oh, that's just a term of endearment."

"So, you deny being the leader of this whole operation?"

"What operation?"

"What operation. Ha, ha, ha!" the man turned to the two-way mirror with a canny laugh. There was a knocking at the two-way mirror. The man rose and left the room. Through the door's narrow, rectangular window, Adam could see a consultation in undertones between that man and a woman in a black suit.

The man came back to the room downtrodden, staggering, with strangely puzzled eyes. He grasped for a chair, flopped onto it, and covered up his eyes with a hand; he groaned, painfully. "Our *very liberal* prime minister has decided to *intervene in your case*," he said in vexation; sneering; his face turning as red as a beet. "He has even sent men—" he twisted to the door then back and pointed to it with a thumb "—*that woman*" (no one was at the door then) "to take you to him." He glared at Adam in a silent stare of a vindictive light; so long that Adam fidgeted in his seat and blinked away. Adam could tell the man wanted, dreadfully, to strike him: to attack; his left eye twitched, with a deep wrinkle between his dark brows. In silence, they scanned each other for a beat. Suddenly, as though he'd studied Adam long enough and could take it no more, the man amply lunged over the table and grasped Adam's neck with two hands and began to wring it.

"You! You! *Traitor!*" he shrieked and wrung Adam's neck. The door flung open. All stormed in in a terrible outcry.

Several men in black positively seized hold of the man and wrestled him off in an argy-bargy of curses, scraping table and chairs. The woman in black suit yanked Adam by the elbow and whisked him off to a waiting car: to the Prime Minister's Office.

~

Adam was sitting outside of the Prime Minister's Office when he saw a man in a red suit with a white trim walk by in a bouncing gait as he gave Adam a fleeting look; followed by a woman in a white dress, red high heels, big, red-rimmed glasses, and hair of a dark brown pulled up tight to a bun. At some distance, the man suddenly stopped; the woman, not foreseeing this halt, ran into his back. They turned to each other, spoke, and glanced questioningly at Adam. Adam realized they were talking about him and eyed the two cunningly. In a flash, Adam recognized the man as Pierre Elliott Trudeau, the two-time prime minister of Canada, as he pirouetted to his office. The woman went up to Adam in high-heeled *click-clacks* which ricocheted up the commodious marble hall. "*Bonjour*," she said with a French shade. "I'm the PM's chief of staff. Mr Adamah, is it?" (She did not wait for a reply.) The PM will see you now."

As Adam walked in the office Mr Trudeau was doing handstand push-ups with the toes of his colourful socks against a wall.

"*Salut, monsieur Adamah*. Hello. *C'est très bien aimable à vous d'être venu nous voir*. It's very nice of you to have come to see us," said Pierre Trudeau as he deftly flipped to his feet and stretched out a hand. Adam shook hands while he thought about what he should be saying, for so long that he ended up saying nothing at all.

"*Cette vilaine guerre! On dirait que le monde entier a perdu la tête*," Pierre Trudeau exclaimed as he went to sit behind his desk.

"Sorry. I don't speak French."

"*Ah! excuses*. I said, what a nasty war..." He motioned to the chairs in front of his desk. "*Asseyez-vous, s'il vous plait. Causons.*

Sit." Adam sat; the chair had extremely high handles, so that he did not know what to do with his arms and hands. (Adam was experiencing the awkwardness which comes with meeting great, powerful people—not to mention, a historical figure at that).

Pierre Trudeau fell to thinking as he looked intently at his clasped hands on the table. "Pray tell," he looked up. "How are my sons back in Canada?"

"Good; good—as far as I know... Justin Trudeau gave a nice eulogy at your funeral."

"Ah! Excellent! *Excellent*! He hasn't gotten himself mixed-up in politics, now, has he?"

"No," Adam shook his head, "no; at least, not before I died."

"*Bien, bien. La politique est une sale affaire.* Nasty business: this politics," he waved a hand, as if shooing a mosquito.

What he should have said earlier—say, came to Adam, only then. "Thank you for intervening in my case, Mr Prime Minister."

"No problem. Hope the men weren't too harsh on you," he said. But before Adam could respond, he snapped: "But, we are *at war*. There are a lot of bleeding hearts around. All I can say is, go on, bleed; society's safety is more important than some weak-kneed people who don't like the looks of things. Don't you agree, Mr Adamah?"

"Well—"

"—No doubt, I've spent a great deal of time in ensuring the institutions of freedom—most important philosophical concepts of liberty—are preserved. So, always—at any rate, intellectually, I've had a great deal of respect for liberty and the institutions of freedom, here and on Earth; if that means anything." He was like a wound-up spring.

"Now, in your case," he went on, "I read transcripts of your brunch discussion and have decided you cannot, possibly, be a spy. But a *prophète*..." he held out two wavering hands. "What kind of a prophet would let anyone take him for a ride, eh? Don't get me wrong; beautiful women have hoodwinked us all. I don't blame you. I blame our intelligence agents. I mean, just her name alone was one *énorme* clue. What were they expecting, a wooden horse? *Un cheval de bois! Aïe!*"

Then the chief of staff snuck her head through the door. The Prime Minister jumped to his feet and bounced to the door. But he stopped at the doorway and turned to Adam, and said: "Well, come along." The PM held an arm out as Adam went to the door, draped it round his shoulders, and gave Adam a hearty shake.

"*Vous vous enrôlez pour la guerre, mon prophète*," he said to Adam. Adam gave a weak nod. (He had no idea what the Prime Minister had said to him.) "Put up your dukes! We are going to beat 'em to the punch," he said, then bobbed and weaved ahead of Adam, as they went to a meeting room, with a "*One-two! One-two!*"

Gathered in the big meeting room were the Prime Minister, his chief of staff, the minister of defence, generals, admirals, and the security bureaus. Adam, at the behest of the Prime Minister, sat in the big meeting room, at the back; by a wall of a humongous, marvellous seismic tomography map of that planet, showing an outer crust, an inner core, and a mantle layered like an onion. In the mantle, at the thousand-kilometer level, two colossal, lump-like blobs—with seas, landmasses, and mountain ranges—bubble up. Together, the superstructures look like bulging onions in the ground with complex root systems branching up to the sub-surface, lengthways and transversely, in a zigzag fashion. But what was like a medley of roots were spaciously branching sub-terranean tunnels and rivers, tangled and crisscrossed in the vast cavernous depths; burrowing side-passages, this way and that; bifurcating; turning obliquely; curling back over themselves, or to chambers and, or dead ends. Those mammoth vacuums and ramifying, many-tunnelled formations were bewildering beyond the coinage of new words. At its topmost, the map picturesquely inked land and waters; above it all, an ocean circumscribing the whole of the globe; and, at its apex, the gyratory motion of seven maëlströms spinning down to the ocean basin and out as seven waterspouts to Necropolis. Black elevation lines blanketed the map along with tightly packed red isobaric lines converging on the ströms and the spouts. Block lettering named the blobs as: "THE HALLEY BLOB" and "THE VERNE BLOB". Red arrows marked: the Halley Blob with "YOU'RE HERE!", "THE NORTHERN ENTRY", and "THE SOUTHERN EXIT". Black skull and crossbones warned: "DANGER: CAVE-IN"; "CHASM"; "RAPIDS"; "IMPASSABLE".

All had arrived at the appointed time. A smell of onions infused the room. "Let us begin," said the chief of staff; who then went through everything having to do with the procedures of the committee's session; and, at some length, declared in a quorum; then called on the minister of defence to provide a latest update. The minister of defence—a Sikh sporting a pointy auburn beard and a big orange turban—held a paper over his lap with his chin on his neck; he was asleep. The chief of staff bent her head down to him and called out his name. He woke from his catnap in a jolt, looked round with puzzled eyes, and then tried to affect an air of nonchalance. She, again, asked him for a briefing. He cleared his throat, wiped his mouth, rose, half asleep, schlepped over to the big map, and began to speak in a monotonous tone while jabbing the map with a long wooden pointer.

"At seventeen hundred, operatives collapsed the—" he hit the map, "—Necropolis Foxhole Pass."

"Did they catch her, the spy?" interrupted a general in low-pitched voice; squeezed into sparkling, medalled green uniform; frowning in Adam's direction with bristling black brows.

The minister of defence, nodding his head, said "No".

"Do you think they'll catch her?"

The minister of defence, shaking his head, said "Yes".

(Adam thought the minister of defence had it all wrong: in that, he should be shaking head when saying no and nodding for yes.)

"Why are you so sure they will catch up to her?" the general asked.

The minister of defence became quite cross. "I am not *so sure* of *nothing!*" he cried, googly-eyed, with a wobbly head. "I kindly ask you, sir, to not put words in my mouth," he kept on wobbling his head. (Adam thought the minister of defence did that right.) The general turned red and shrugged his shoulders sneeringly.

The room fell silent. Somebody wanting to pass gas silently let out a squeaker. The chief of staff rubbed her nose with a long finger.

"Isn't government fun?" asked the Prime Minister. "*Ne perdons point de temps.* To make the meeting productive, I ask you all to listen, and to ask pertinent questions." Then, addressing the minister of defence, he wondered: "Could she have gotten out?"

"Our fastest climbers have clocked a time of over thirty-six hours. A boy saw a woman go in the caves—" he poked the map, "—at noon yesterday."

"So, she's trapped in there."

"Yes."

"*C'est bien, c'est bien...*"

On hearing the great news on Sinon, Adam was truly downcast about it. The thought of her suffering in that dark, cramped labyrinth stabbed his heart much more than her treachery. Somehow, Adam, still, cared for her.

"Don't think it makes any difference," said an admiral, with a pale face and a bland voice, in a white, medalled uniform. "We must assume she was monitored on the way, and that they now know our general location; *et tout ce qui s'en suit.*"

"We received intel on movements of TBMs (Tunnel Boring Machines)—moles, two days ago," said a man in a black suit and sunglasses. The defence minister struck the map with his pointer.

"*Y a-t-il de l'espoir? Is there any hope?*" cried the army general in both of the official languages.

"*Parlons raison; reason over passion,*" the Prime Minister said. Then asked the defence minister: "How quickly can these moles dig?"

"Ten to fifty feet per day to several hundred feet per day."

"Why such a big range?"

"Because the thing that'll slow them down is not those fast-moving moles but *mucking*: the removal of all the dirt and rock."

"What's the fastest that they can reach the closest tunnels?"

"Those giant augers could dig a fifteen-foot-diameter shaft in..." he stroked his beard, turned and drew out the division with his pointer on the map, carrying the ones and twos, and declared: "...in six months."

The prime Minister and the admiral exchanged a stare.

"*Mon Dieu!*" exclaimed the army general. "*My God!*"

"*Soyez homme! A man!*" the Prime Minister chided.

The admiral snorted at the general, and, scornfully, looked away. The minister of defence had a hard time stifling his yawns.

The rest of the company around the table were obstinately silent, and had been, as oft happens in all meetings, throughout. They were, likely, ones concerned only with personal interests:

promotions, raises. Somewhere along the way they had learned: for success you do not need intelligence, nor hard work, but only a talent for carrying water for those with power who reward unquestioning service. So, in meetings they keep their mouth shut and, from time to time, nod at superiors in agreement; and when directed to do anything—wrong, immoral, and otherwise—they bow head and say "Yes—sir".

"Must square off the army, at once! We'll flank them! Outflank them!" aired the general, with a frightened face.

The Prime Minister and the admiral exchanged intent looks, once more, expressive of some secret complicity.

The Prime Minister rubbed his face and eyes with his hands; then stood, paced the room, stopped, gestured at the general, and said: "We started to win this war once we lost conventional warfare and began to employ guerrilla tactics. Even if we could scare up a hundred thousand men to bare-knuckle a conventional war, again, it'd be futile: we don't have tanks, fighter jets..., etcetera."

"With all due respect, are you suggesting we sit here and do *nothing?*"

"*Tout vient à celui qui sait attendre.* (Everything comes to ones who know how to wait.) Patience and time," the Prime Minister quoted Tolstoy. "What we do have are three destroyers, and..., a prophet," he pointed to Adam. Adam blushed hot at all the eyes.

"You cannot be serious!" the general mocked. "The man is crazy," he shot Adam a scornful smile, eyeing the Prime Minister with an insolent scowl, pushing his chair back and reclining into it, airily, with an insulting, groping, contemptuous composure. Adam turned his nose up in a smirk, revealing his missing tooth.

An angry glint lit up in the Prime Minister's eyes. He looked the general directly in the face as though he saw right thorough the man. "That kind of intemperate language is Goebbels's well-known technique, to degrade. We will win wars with moral superiority, and with that special, elusive quintessence known as *spirit*." He pointed at Adam. "Now, this man may very well be crazy—and after this is all said and done, I plan to drill him on philosophy, religion, quantum mechanics, and to debate him on theological challenges, around the dinner table—but it is just his craziness that is what's needed now. People need to believe in a force higher than themselves. They haven't heard him speak—all they know is that his birth has fulfilled some prophecy—but they *believe*." The Prime Minister gave the admiral a meaningful nod. "And just as the enemy hit us a low below by using this man to smuggle their spy into our midst, we will use him to strike them at *their* Cole-prophet's lair. As so, we will lead with our chin."

The admiral spread a sketch of the Sky Ocean on the table, which depicted a needle-like tower amidst a ring of seven ströms. The red tower, the ströms, and the spaces between them all had measurements, barometric pressure gradients, wind speeds, and wave heights tantamount to cliffs. The graphic had a red title of: ISSACHAR'S TOWER.

The admiral took out a picture of a portrait that Adam had seen in the warden's office and said: "We have all seen paintings of this man with his face concealed by rings of fire and hear the fantastical tales of a necromancer with an army of Red Dragons." (Adam lifted by this unexpected twist the meeting was taking.) "We had dismissed them as Goebbels concocted fantasies for his sadistic war propaganda. Sometime ago our friends at CSIS," he peeped at the man in the sunglasses, "informed us the anecdotes were not the imaginings of that sick and perverted man but *very* real. CSIS has a highly placed informant inside Hitler's Office of the Führer. And suffice it to say, in such-and-such a way, this So-and-So *une telle* was able to pass on this photocopy of the long-rumoured Issachar Tower. At twelve hundred hours two frigates will set sail to attack and destroy the tower." He looked over at the minister of defence, and then added: "At the strict order of the minister of defence." As though awakening from a reverie, the minister of defence revived with a sort of exacerbation and smacked the map with a backslash of his pointer—*thwack*—and gave himself a scare.

"How long will the voyage take?" asked the Prime Minister.

"At maximum speed," the admiral bent a finger of one hand with a finger of his other hand; "at thirty knots," he bent another finger; "five and a half months, or so," he waved an arm, vaguely.

"Cutting it tight... *Qui vivra verra*, time will tell," he intoned.

The general cackled. "Have you lost your minds? These are dubious, fanciful, children's bedtime hocus-pocus stories."

"Don't know about this Issachar dude, but I can attest to the existence of the Red Dragons," Adam said. "While escaping I was hunted by four of them—else, it was two, twice," Adam eyed left in wondering.

The general, with his smug countenance, fumbled about his crotch under his big, leaning belly.

"All settled...?" asked the Prime Minister. "*Allons, vite, vite!*" He slapped the admiral on the back. "I will give you my personal photographer to capture it all blow-by-blow; and great pics of Mr Adamah on the frigates," he said, and snapped his fingers in glee.

"*Me!*" cried Adam, springing to feet as dogs do at times for walks.

"I'm giving you a ringside seat!" the Prime Minister yanked Adam by the back of the neck and began to walk out with him. "I am enlisting you in the war effort. Wars are won with the *spirit* of the men; who better to give that to them? But *entre nous*, try to not speak; the more mysterious you are the better, *mon prophète*."

"But—"

"—No buts! It is the least you can do to make up for giving up our location to the enemy... Take it on the chin." He turned to the admiral. "If you capture this Issachar fellow, alive, need great pics of you two standing over him after the knockout blow. Give 'em a good sucker punch, straight from the shoulder—don't pull your punches. The gloves are off. If need be, go down swinging." He added, "But no risqué photographs," as an afterthought.

"We'll do, sir."

They were about to leave the room when the prime minister pulled Adam aside. And he whispered, "How come God brings so much death, destruction, and misery?"

"It's not God! there's no darkness in Him at all. Light has no communion with darkness."

"Why does He allow it then. Why doesn't He do anything?"

"He cannot—at least, not directly; else, He'd be sullied, too. He needs a bridge—someone to achieve spiritual understanding, first—the understanding Jesus had; then He can act, via *that* consciousness bridge."

"*Vous êtes une fine mouche.* Was expecting God works in mysterious ways..."

As Adam and the prime minister were exiting the doorway, Adam looked back.

The army general, ambling about, stopped behind the chief of staff, squeezed her shoulders for a massage. She recoiled from his gropes. He drew back his hands and left the room.

The minister of defence was trying to lean the long pointer on the map with nervous hands; he managed to prop the pointer on the map, took one step, the pointer slew and fell with a *spank*, and the minister of defence hop-skipped away.

Chapter Seven

Second Death

PING, PING, *ping*, *Charon's* sonar sounded out, ceaselessly; each *ping* succeeding, before its echo faded away, by a further ringing *ping*; and then, by another, and another. The sea heaved and the steel-grey ship rose and fell beneath Adam's wet feet.

"Sonar contact, bearing zero niner zero. Range six, six, six."

On the bridge the captain picked up his binoculars hung on his neck and trained them to the starboard port side.

"Right neatly to course zero niner zero."

"Right neatly to course zero niner zero. Aye-aye, sir."

Charon leaned deep over to starboard as she turned. Waves broke against the ship and cascaded as though off a cliff. Adam's feet shot from under him, his wet hands lost their grip over a rail, he slid the opposite way and flitted feetfirst upon the captain.

"You shouldn't be on this bridge," cried the mad captain.

That was true. Adam should not have been on that bridge. He had begun the journey on *Charon's* sister escort ship, the *Styx*.

Six months ago, men in black ushered Adam and the prime minister's photographer to a seaport, then to the destroyers with the secret mission of obliterating Issachar Tower. For their send-off, the crowd gathered had raised on tiptoe while waving handkerchiefs in a prolonged, tear-filled hail of farewells. Before that they had fell silent and pushed apart to make way as Adam and his entourage moved in through them. Adam was not expecting anyone was to see him off. Then Mary jostled out from the crush.

"I have a confession to make," she said in a hurry.

"What is it?"

"Wanted to tell you. That whole brain surgery thing is a big head fake. It's the placebo effect which brings to mind a person's past life on Earth." She pursed her lips. "We go thru the *motions* of an operation, with actors. Belief in brain surgery plays the big trick." Adam told her that that was a clever bit of work: something from nothing, as a hand plucked him back and away from her.

The striking ships, cut like elongated canoes, had helicopter decks and twin fifty-calibre guns at bows. Their funnels, erected in blocks, had sexangular bridges with angled out windows and antenna towers of various dish radars whirling round and round. Depth charge throwers were on the beams and astern. And giant-sized binoculars and machineguns flanked at astern and on the bows. The two warships rocked and creaked against their ropes.

A navy band staged a jingle. The frigate captains saluted the Admiral and stepped aside and tailed behind as he inspected the four hundred sailors that stood at attention and in rank. And the Admiral gave an admirable speech on good and evil, mentioning Adam, in passing, as a spiritual guide in their journey. At the end of his speech the sailors bawled out a strong, extended "Hura-a-ah!"

The frigates set off (on Operation Sheitaan), with a supply-and-refuelling ship, to the edge of the inner sea; then, via canals and locks, to a titanic lava chimney (with gigantic rock walls that rose to a drawn-out arch) which led out of a ridge at the edge of the Sky Ocean.

Those ships had two main gangways, one on each side, with connecting passages; with easy to get to cables, ducts, and panels for fixes and upkeep; with steep, narrow, ladder-like stairs. Thick steel doors seal off sections and corridors (flats). Bar for one port-hole in the captain's quarters there are no windows below decks. The galley sat in the middle of the messes; and the ranks had their own messes, which branch to cross passages. And, they had their own living quarters. Senior officers stretched single cabins. Petty officers occupied six berth cabins; juniors shared spaces that slept twelve; with bunks, stacked in threes, having ten inches between the racks and cobalt curtains across them; and small washrooms, with four showers, shared by fifty men. Adam had the luxury of his own cabin and a senior officers' benefit of larger washrooms. (Unbeknownst to him, the captain—blue-eyed and level-headed, able to assess all situations and make definitive decisions—willy-nilly, took Adam as for a chaplain; and expected Sunday sermons and for Adam to preside over ceremonies such as burials at sea.)

The claustrophobic life on the *Styx* started before dawn with the officer of the watch blowing an ear-piercing whistle thru the speakers, with a teasing "Wakey-wakey"; exercises below decks; breakfast; and a chopper launch to patrol the waters all-round. The sailors on a watch were on twelve hour rotating shifts; they spent the rest of their time playing cards, chatting, and sleeping.

A sun shone red-hot over that ocean—too brightly; Erath's ghost sun is much bigger, and a lot hotter—scorching. The look-outs and other sailors on the decks wore shiny protective suits.

The final dawn crept in with the sky shell-pink on only one side. The ships lulled listlessly on nine-foot-high swells. An ill, backing wind shook a leg south-southeast, counterclockwise, as an outlying tap of a low-pressure cyclone. The sea had taken on a greyish, marbled sheen like that of a bad red meat. A warble of static came out of the speakers throughout.

By then their flotilla of three ships had sailed, sailed, sailed over that ocean, straight up and straight down, for one hundred and eighty days: facing not a single enemy combat ship nor submarine. They spent the days, one after another, in rambling hearsay; about their intelligence—or lack thereof—of such folly, such a misadventure, and, for so long; and, over what? some tricksy informant? But that kind of animated gossip was only amongst the junior officers. (Adam liked to spend all his time with them: the common folk, the working stiff.) There was no gossip among the senior officers, like that, since speaking those sorts of things was not the right thing to do; besides, they believed the enemy did not patrol the ocean, lock, stock and barrel, since they would suppose the Underground incapable of reaching the Sky Ocean. The junior officers, on the other hand, wondered how the enemy was able to get to it.

"They use an underground passage, maybe, like us."

"Then they know about the hollows? They would've deep-sixed us, by now."

"Not necessarily."

"O, sod off."

"I'm serious."

"Hardy-har-har! Beat it."

"It's the necromancer," chimed in another, with a voice high in excitement; "they say he is a wizard. Sorcerers can do all kinds of occult magical thingumajigs."

"They snap their ships and themselves up here, in a poof?"

"Why not?"

"Why not! Ya; that old hag puts them up here. Blockhead."

Adam snapped a head from one to the other as though there were no telling what he might hear from each of them.

"What you think, Chaplain. Think that ol' shrew has power like that?" (Over those long months their tone toward Adam had taken on a less formal nature.)

"Which old shrew?"

"The Devil, I reckon. *Fra Diavolo*."

"Surely you don't believe in mumbo-jumbo Devil, after all."

"Oh, *pshaw*! Who can believe in *him*? Though, he does seem real..."

"Oh, for shame, guys. For shame!" Adam had spent a whole sermon on debunking the Devil, Satan; and thought that he had succeeded, with the use of logic, reason, and copious quotes from the Bible; for which the captain had summoned him to his quarters to give him a proper talking-to. And that was the following time. The first time the captain had summoned him to his quarters came to pass immediately following Adam's initial Sunday sermon. Adam figured it was a great idea to start with preaching against public prayers. Quoting Jesus as saying, to be not as the hypocrites are: for they love to pray standing in churches and in the corners of the streets so that others may see them. And to not use vain repetitions, as the heathen do: for they think that God will hear them for their much speaking. And to not ask for *anything*, even, because one cannot inform God of nothing He does not already know; since, "God knows what things ye have need of, before you ask him". For that, the captain, who sat front row centre, with eyes staring out of his head, gave Adam a dressing-down.

On that last day, the three ships rolled and pitched as they never rolled and pitched before, rising and falling in fountains of spray. They were heading right into a terrific storm of towering, dark cumulus clouds; with lightning flushing and branching out in the thunderclouds; like how an aeroplane flies from clear skies into a thunderstorm.

Bells hammered in *ring, ring, ring*. From loudspeakers came the captain's voice ordering general quarters. Horns blared. Each man rushed to a post: an outburst of boots up and down ladders. In a bat of an eye Adam sat on his own in the junior officers' mess, with a strewn chess set and play cards, and the remains of a half-eaten meal. Someone, off in his socks, had left his running shoes.

"Now hear this. Now hear this. This is your captain. We are homing in on target. Expect heavy resistance. Look alive."

Speakers squawked the ship's communications.

"Sonar contact, bearing two seven zero."

"Range?"

"Range one thousand; closing."

"Left to course two seven zero."

"Left to course two seven zero. Aye-aye, sir."

A sub lay a thousand yards from them, broad on port beam; perhaps.

"Request permission to attack."

"Request granted."

"Left standard rudder. Twelve knots."

"Left standard rudder. Twelve knots. Aye-aye, sir."

The ship vibrated. The plates, utensils, and chess pieces rattled.

"Control room reports twelve knots, sir."

Adam became conscious of the sonar's droning pings. Over the months Adam had become accustomed to that *ping-ping-ping,* like unmindfulness of *ding, ding, ding* of slot machines in a casino after only a few minutes.

He heard three thuds: from the back, then, one on each side.

He felt keyed up. Something heavy throbbed, beat against the ship's walls and the floor... (It was his own pounding heart.)

"We're coming half-cocked, sir."

"Right full rudder!"

"Right full rudder. Aye-aye, sir."

"All engines flank speed."

"Aye-aye. All engines flank speed."

"Control room reports flank speed, sir."

The engines' pulses went up his feet, shook his guts, tremored in his skull; the ship's stern dropped, bow lifted, it lurched, inclined sharply, and tilted to over forty-five degrees; and sent Adam and tables and chairs and the plates in the galley flying and smashing to a side. Then, the unthinkable: the ship skimmed backwards; then, flipped end over end: pitch-poled! stem to stern, stem to stern, stem to stern; Adam tossed head to toe, head to toe, head to toe; flung against bulkheads; in a landslide of bits and pieces and running shoes.

"ALL HANDS ABANDON SHIP! ALL HANDS ABANDON SHIP!"

(Endeavouring to mount a sharp wave the ship had slipped back down, its stern had buried itself in the wave's trough, and the crest of the wave had caught the ship's bow and flipped her over.)

There was a buckling trill crunch. With horrified eyes Adam looked on as the ship's steel bolts sheared and popped out. Steel bulkheads exploded. The inrushing tens of tons of jetting water rushed in a great woosh, tore in through walls, coursed compartments, inundated all the quarters, and killed the engines, in mere seconds.

Clicking lights blinked off. Blue sparks arced and forked in the water; and the ship's electrical system shorted out to absolute darkness.

The ship oscillated now, hull up: inverted. In an air pocket, sounds were blunt, deadened. Water came up hard, and fast—to his waist—to his chest—his chin. Habituated to thrashings, pitch-black, and nerve-wracking plights, Adam kept a cool head. He took in deep breaths and timed his last breath as water engulfed him. Submerged, he attempted to break out with that one lungful of air. He swam down along a hull and through a blown aft hatch out from under the ship, and at once kicked out to get to the surface. His chest and throat convulsed as he swallowed in urges to take a breath; it was like vice grips squeezed his lungs to a breakpoint.

Bodies drifted all over, suspended open-eyed.

He burst out gasping to a shrieking darkness and foaming, chaotic waters. The sea heaped, slammed together, and moved apart, every which way. A yellow raft cartwheeled over his head. Screaming winds hurled water at his face. So much water stirred in the air that he near drowned from breathing. He rose and fell, rose and fell with enormous, rolling waves. Life buoy flares were aflare, and a searchlight combed the foam-streaked combers. To one side, bluish red fire shot from a blast of a blinding explosion. *Styx* blew. Flaming shards flew—catapulted. Thick smoke mushroomed. A shockwave walloped. The ship listed up, and the deep ingested her in a tizzy of sizzling, smothering huffing and puffs.

A shout he heard—maybe; the screeching wind drowned it. He scanned the horizon and saw a dark shape on the inky surface of the sea. Survivors! on a fragment of the wreckage; appearing-disappearing behind swelling walls of water. (Out of sight when inside troughs, visible atop crests, then out of view another time.)

Waves rolled o'er from every side. With each superseding wave swooping them apart, then swinging them close; with a dragged-out hundred-foot crest-to-trough undulation in-between. On his next tip top, a helicopter hovers over the men with its searchlight spotting a cone of light; blades whipping out leaf-shaped ripples round the two seamen. He resolves he must go swim out to them. Easily thought than done; the seas are so massive he fancies he is swimming up a mountain and down some peak. And after a few moments of solid effort, he gave up: in seeing that he had drew farther away. Yet, in two shakes, a roller picked him up and set him right beneath the helicopter, stupendously. Sporting night-vision spectacles, the helicopter pilot strove to keep up a sixty-foot hover, but the roaring downpour kept pelting him down-ward. Adam swam to the sailors, which held onto a blown hatch for dear life. "CHAPLAIN! YOU MADE IT!" yelled one of the men. He could not recognize those two men: they looked like soaking wet cats. A figure in a black wetsuit with a hood, fins, and snorkel gear jumped from the helicopter with his hands to his sides. He swam—slashed across the crests, with ease, on the face of it. He come about Adam and the men, then shouted, "HELLO! I'M HERE TO RESCUE—" The chopper's co-pilot pushed a life basket down. The rescue swimmer asked who is going first and Adam pointed to one of the men with a nasty scarlet gash on his kisser. The lift bucket bucked at the typhoon-force wind. They got into the hoist basket, one by limp one—like albatrosses; tussled in one leg by another—then went up, one after the other; with sixty-foot seas burying them in long-winded dunks as they surged out and up.

The in-water rescue went swimmingly; they were inside the helicopter and wrapped up in shiny blankets. The pilot tilted the chopper's nose down to the command ship *Charon*. On approach, Adam could see *Charon's* shimmering lights rise and fall in the dappled gloom. Squalls carpeted the windshield in an onslaught, en route. Gale-force howling winds blew the chopper backwards. However, after a country mile, they made it to the ship. The pilot placed the helipad at his six o'clock, hovered low and the co-pilot paid out the haul-down cable to a sailor on deck which snatched the cable and secured it on the beartrap. But before the beartrap-assisted landing kicked in to pull the helicopter down to clamp it with its jaws, a hundred-foot wave across the bow bashed in the helicopter onto the deck and drove it toward the edge of the ship; with its blades and tail rotors slashing the deck in a fever pitch of *clip-clop-clip-clop-clip-clop* sparks. It jetted into the ship's railing—discharging its passengers into the splashing sea as it went over the edge—its tail snagged the rails; and, in a finale, it yawned at the side of a plunging *Charon* in leftover flying from its mangled, sagging blades; with the mutilated torsos of the pilot and the co-pilot dangling out of the shattered bloodied windshield.

Tchah! Adam found himself bowled into the boisterous, ballooning sea, once again. Driven sheeters lashed his face. The billowing seas devoured space. Surf thundered *Charon* in tempo; in headstrong fury; one arising out of another in a continual churn. White-water pillars cast skyward showers on *Charon*. That bloating sea uplifted him in an upward flight some two hundred feet above the ship—wavered—then, dropped him two hundred feet below the ship. The swarming blizzard no longer screamed nor shrieked but moaned. *Charon's* scramble-nets were down, searchlights running; one of the beams passed Adam over, but then seesawed back and pried directly at him. The downfall zipped by in the limelight horizontally. He receded and advanced to and from the ship. He took to pinch the scramble-nets at each sway's yo-yo. A prolonged exertion ensued: culminating in a crescendo of a vehement falsetto cry as he clinched a net's bosom, at last.

He looked keenly around for the sailors that had gone overboard with him but could not see them. As he clambered up the net, he saw the photographer, in a yellow raingear and lifejacket, rather than bearing a hand, taking his picture.

~

"You shouldn't be on this bridge," cried the mad captain.

"I was told you'd asked to see me."

"Right... What happened on the *Styx*? Where's the tanker?"

Adam—wrapped in a green blanked, with the black tuque on his head, still, drooping and dripping—puckered his lips and shrugged his shoulders, and said, "Don't know."

The captain—a dour, middle-aged man with a reddish hair, nimbly balanced on his bony legs—gave Adam a withering stare. "*Hmph*," he exhaled, and rubbed his head.

"Sir. Ops reports all bogeys vanished."

The captain, at a loss, sniffed; his lips twitched with anger.

"Sir. Ops reports all instruments bogged down with static."

A flitting, flashing swell thrust them up high, then, dropped out from under them. The captain and Adam crouched, extended their arms out, gymnast-style, steadied, then lifted back up.

"What about that tower?" asked the grimacing captain.

"Lookouts see no tower, sir."

The captain took his cap and whacked it on the floor. "Been chasing orchestrated shadows! Phantoms! A bogeyman. There is *no* tower, *no* subs." After an inner labour to compose, he charged: "I want to know how much longer till the chopper is cut."

"Aye-aye, captain. How long till the chopper is cut."

"Ensure all hatches are battened," he ordered another.

"Ensure all hatches are battened. Aye-aye, sir."

"And turn that bleeping bleeping off," he balked at a third.

"And turn that bleeping bleeping off. Aye-aye, sir."

Outside in the opaque darkness the wind moaned no more; it made an eery, deep, tonal resonance with the ship's cables, like a pipe organ being played by a rascally cat that was walking on it.

"Right to course one eight zero. We're going home."

"Right to course one eight zero. Aye-aye, sir."

Spray soared abaft. Adam, by the door of the bridge, shimmying, got a hold of its handle. *Charon's* abrupt turn had brought her in the sink of a roaring roller short of rising to it. She dipped, askew for a scary moment; then, went atilt the other way, for another frightful moment, before righting herself in verso, punch-drunk.

"Stem the tide."

"Stem the tide. Aye-aye, sir."

The captain went to the radio and broadcasted, "All hands on deck. All hands on deck."

As the captain dished out his commands, from one to the other, his eye glided over Adam. At last, he turned to Adam and said, "Look at me. Look at me—" he drew forked fingers over his eyes. "—here. What are you, still, doing on my bridge? Get out!"

Adam had been dilly-dallying because he did *not* want to go out on that deck to get below decks; it was fearsome out there! Bursts crashed–crashed on that door, made it quake, and drove up its hinges. He waved to a door rear of the captain's chair and asked, "May I go down in through that door there?"

"*Pff...* That goes to Operations Room. No!"

"What about that other door, beside it, there?"

"That goes to Engineering Control. Get out!" He pointed up and over, all hoity-toity, with eyebrows arching commandingly.

Adam squinted out of the bridge door's window. A hodge-podge, ad hoc group of men were struggling to free the downed chopper from the deck's rails with a chainsaw; the photographer took pics. Adam was shilly-shallying when, a breaker swept the deck. *Charon* went into a three-hundred-and-sixty-degree barrel roll, with every body on the bridge tumbling, and climbed out of the foam. All on deck, save for the photographer, had went overboard.

Everyone pushed themselves up who still could and clawed back to their stations, nursing cuts and bruises.

"Gone overboard! Gone overboard!"

"All engines full stop."

"All engines full stop. Aye-aye, sir."

"Engine room reports all engines stopped, sir."

"All engines back one-third."

"All engines back one-third. Aye-aye, sir."

"Engine room reports all engines back one-third, sir."

"Wheel about."

"Wheel about. Aye-aye, sir."

Charon came about her own wake in a convolution, heeling a sharp turn, wallowing in a queasy motion, with seas socking her awash in spray from some heavy hitters. But she was even-keeled. She ducked it out; each time picking herself up like a demented, shirtless man gunning out of a rollover in a police chase. As *Charon* rotated, a swell rose up to their front like a mountain: a near vertical freak with a crest of white waterfalls like moonlit clouds.

"Dead ahead! Dead ahead!"

"All engines flank speed!" The captain was going to climb that thing.

"All engines flank speed. Aye-aye, sir."

Charon waltzed on up the sheer face of that non-negotiable billow in an agonizingly slow upsurge and with juddering effort. They were all transfixed and white-knuckled-gripped. For a hair-raising moment it looked as though they were not going to make it. *Charon* ebbed and flowed in neck-snapping vibrations akin to a launching space shuttle.

They made the peak! All jumped to feet with extended fists with a "YAH!" like a tipsy bar crowd behind a scoring home team.

Charon roller-coastered, and then, tipped the wave's tip: to a hole in the ocean. They did not surf down the face of that wave, because it just left out from under them; they nosedived into the thickening black, parting abyss at a skreiching terminal velocity.

The ensemble on the bridge let slip long-drawn-out screams at highest octaves while goggling at the angled windows and one another:

"AAA...—AAA..."

What they were all thinking was self-evident: A long way down!

They fisted the well's keister like hammering into a concrete slab. The ship squished—like how high calibre bullets flatten on impact with water—Adam and the crew shot out from exploding windows—the squashed *Charon* took a dive; with Adam pinned against the aft rails, in immense pressure change which deafened him.

Argh! He was down and out this time: it was too far to reach the surface. But, after thinking about it, he thought, that, perhaps, he was only, as yet, down and out for the count; that he can *pray*. He had not breathed for so long that he was reaching the break-point: a hundred and forty seconds. The dark closed in from all sides. "Cannot die, now. Never found out who is that cat shape-shifter. And Sinon—" An involuntary trigger opened his mouth.

He breathed in water; a spasmodic breath dragged water into his windpipe, tickled his vocal cords, and triggered his larynx to contract; and he began to drown without water in his lungs: to suffocate.

He prayed: This is a dream. None of it is real. I'm not in this dream.

Human consciousness is the father of itself, because: it is ignorant of the fact that consciousness projects everything; fear of not seeing how things come about; and, as a result, its made-up rules and laws, causes and effects. While, all the while, it is human consciousness itself that is projecting all that it fears and believes.

When I realize I am dreaming—have lucid dreams, my real consciousness takes over and the consciousness that is making up the dream can no longer project itself, and I wake up. I'm in pure consciousness, now. Outside looking in. I am *not* in this body; therefore, I *cannot* die.

He hears a voice call his name.
He knows that voice...
He opens his eyes. He is looking up at Flora!

www.ingramcontent.com/pod-product-compliance
Lightning Source LLC
Chambersburg PA
CBHW010511100726
47902CB00011B/2169